OVERSEAS SERVICE

by

J. C. Ladenheim

HERITAGE BOOKS
2018

HERITAGE BOOKS

AN IMPRINT OF HERITAGE BOOKS, INC.

Books, CDs, and more—Worldwide

For our listing of thousands of titles see our website
at
www.HeritageBooks.com

Published 2018 by
HERITAGE BOOKS, INC.
Publishing Division
5810 Ruatan Street
Berwyn Heights, Md. 20740

Heritage Books by the author:

Abe Lincoln Afloat

Alien Horseman: An Italian Shavetail with Custer

Custer's Thorn: The Life of Frederick W. Benteen

Grant's Keeper: The Life of John A. Rawlins

The Jarrett-Palmer Express of 1876: Coast to Coast in Eighty-three Hours

Lincoln and Emancipation in the District of Columbia

Overseas Service

International Standard Book Number
Paperbound: 978-0-7884-5855-2

Table of Contents

INTRODUCTION v

PREFACE ix

MILITARY ATTACHÉ 1

TANK COMMANDER 185

DEPUTY COMMANDANT 266

POSTLUDE 297

ACKNOWLEDGEMENTS 298

AUTHOR'S NOTE

Apart from well-known and immediately recognizable public figures, most other characters in this story are drawn from the imagination. There is no General Manning, or Manning Trust, or Manning Mansion, nor is it the desire of the author to demean, criticize or ridicule any member of the armed services or diplomatic service. The author denies an intent to ridicule General Patton, but reminds the reader that every citizen of this great country is entitled to his (or her) own opinion.

INTRODUCTION

I have been asked to include an account of how these rather peculiar chronicles came to be published.

As the most junior member of my law firm, I was instructed to go to the Manning Mansion and close out the "remainders." The antiques, furnishings and laboratory equipment had already been disposed of. My job was to see that nothing else of value had previously escaped attention.

Somewhat resentful, I drove to the mansion situated in southern New Hampshire, just over the Massachusetts border. It had been built originally by the Goodspear family toward the turn of the 20th century and had passed into the possession of the Mannings, who converted one wing into a residence and the remainder into laboratories and offices, to supplement the research activities at Manning Industries, off Kenmore Square in Cambridge, Massachusetts.

I met the on-site supervisor and together we toured the garage, the living quarters above the garage, the out-buildings, the attic and the many rooms of the mansion, without finding anything of value. It was almost as if I had been sent on a fool's errand.

As I prepared to leave, I pointed to pile of coverless books under the *porte cochere* outside the entrance.

"Garbage," the site superintendent assured me. "Nothing of value," He had checked with one of my predecessors and had been told the books could be disposed of, but that the leather covers had to be removed and assigned a monetary value.

I examined the dozen or so books carefully. Most had some rain damage, but the writing was quite legible. The oldest books written in a child's hand appeared to be random observations, the more recent ones dealt with events chronologically presented and were written in an adult script. The volumes with children's writing I discarded, and the rest I loaded into the trunk compartment of my auto, resolving to show them to my wife, who is an assistant professor of history at Tufts University.

Unfortunately, I forgot about the books, until one evening when my front right tire punctured on a road not serviced by Triple A, and I had to remove most of the books before I could access the spare.

When we arrived home, my wife requested that I bring in a few volumes, which I did, after first spreading an old white sheet on our dining room table. After having inspected them, and after searching the contemporary literature on the web, she concluded that the documents had some limited historical interest and that the material dealing with the chronicler's stay in Berlin 1939–41 should certainly be published. There was no peace in our household until I prepared a manuscript of Manning's tour of duty in Berlin, which, at her "suggestion," I showed to my boss, who is the son of the founder of the firm, and a former serving officer on the staff of General Dwight Eisenhower during World War II.

His conclusion was that our firm had an obligation to the deceased and to contemporary scholarship to publish a judicious selection of material relating to his Berlin mission. Concerning the remainder of the chronicles, i.e., the Manning's military experiences with General Patton in the Third Army, he thought they too should be published. When I protested that I lacked the military expertise to undertake this job, he replied that I should proceed as best a layman could, and select only the information that the average reader might understand. This I have tried to do to the best of my very limited ability, but a death in my family has compelled me to turn over this work to another, a historian known to, and recommended by my wife, who promises to bring this work to fruition. All this, in the hope that these chronicles may be "of some interest to the interested reader."

T.W. Coogins, Esq.

PREFACE
By

Colonel F W Holmes USA (Ret.)

I write this critique at the request of my dear friend and former comrade-in-arms, Desmond Everett White II, Esq. It represents my own opinion and, in no regard, reflects that of the U.S. Army.

One has difficulty in assessing the mission of Captain Brian Manning USA in Berlin from 1939–1941. On the one hand, he participated in several important espionage operations of unquestionable value to U.S. Intelligence. He was also instrumental in collecting and relaying important military information to his superiors, while at the same time acquiring a basic knowledge of Panzer operations, which was to serve him and the U.S. Army well during his later service in World War II. Considered in that context, Captain Manning served his country tolerably well in Berlin, and seems to have succeeded (barely) in heeding the one caution assigned to him: stay out of trouble!

His subsequent experiences as tank commander in the Third Army is, likewise, of limited interest, since the account of the 324th Tank Regiment has been replicated in the accounts of other Third Army officers, in closer contact with, and with a greater respect for, the tactical genius of General George S. Patton.

Finally, his brief service in post-war Berlin is of limited military interest, except to note that he did, in fact, help to restore discipline and to smarten up the appearance of the U.S. Berlin Garrison.

I regret I cannot attribute more importance to the notebooks, other than to say that it might be of further interest to readers with a fondness for melodrama.

F.W.H.

MILITARY ATTACHÉ

May 22, 1939

The campus empties quickly, once summer comes to Rousy, Indiana. I was pouring over the syllabuses for the next four ROTC classes, when the mail carrier entered my office and laid a familiar brown envelope on my desk. It was from the US Army Personnel Office, informing me that I was to be relieved of command by a Captain Ralph Pruit on May 24, 1939, and that I was to report to the Deputy Chief of War Plans, War Department, Washington, DC, for further orders.

From the telephone in the outer office, I dialed home and asked Agnes Perkins to send her husband to the ROTC Office. When the m/sergeant arrived, I showed him the letter. He was as astonished as I was. My predecessor had been here 4 years, and I had been here only two. When I asked whether Perkins would be prepared for the turn-over, he assured me that he kept a running inventory and could easily be ready in 45 minutes.

Back at the boarding house, I told Agnes the bad news and had my trunk and valise brought up from the basement. The plan was for me to carry with me in the valise one Class A Uniform and a dark business suit, together with accessories. The remainder was to go into the trunk. The packing went quickly, or as quickly as might be expected, since I have a complete inventory of uniforms, including formal dress uniforms and sword, which I have never worn.

At the end of packing, I picked up a framed photograph of Cynthia, my former fiancée, whom I had met after an Army-Yale football game and courted briefly. She was a Mt. Holyoke student, the daughter of a well-known society couple from New York. Within a remarkably short time after our engagement was announced, she lost interest in the life of an Army wife, and our engagement was abruptly broken, to the profound relief of both of us and her family.

I considered throwing away her picture, but reconsidered, since the frame was sterling silver, and it would take too much time to unbend the nails whose shaft held the photograph in the frame. So, I threw the picture into the trunk.

May 23, 1939

Made the rounds to say my goodbyes to the faculty, but almost all of the department heads and most of the administration had left on vacation. I did see the bursar and asked to be remembered. My recent inamorata, a fresh arrival to the faculty of the English Department, was away in the Gaspé Peninsula for the summer with her new boyfriend.

May 24, 1939

Captain Ralph Pruit showed up in uniform. I had known him from West Point and always found him pleasant. The change of command took only a few minutes. I showed him the roster of ROTC students, and the inventories of the Springfield 03's, the Colt 1911 45's, our old Maxim machine gun (inoperative), etc., and reviewed the syllabuses for next year's classes.

When we had finished, I offered to sell him my 1932 Chevy coupe for $250. The bill of sale was produced, and the car was signed over. Also, I told him about the Perkins boarding house, and he agreed to move into my old room the following day. Meanwhile, he had a room reserved at the hotel for one night.

May 25, 1939

M/Sergeant Perkins and a graduate student helped me load the trunk into his pickup truck, and then Perkins, Aggie and I drove down to the station. I consigned the trunk to the baggage depot at Union Station in Washington and bought a Pullman ticket. For the trip, I wore slacks and polo shirt.

I gave Aggie a hug and thanked her for all she had done for me. For Perkins, I just shook his hand and hoped that it sufficiently conveyed my feelings.

The Pullman passengers seemed to be mostly commercial men, pleasant enough company. We took our meals in the dining car, but most of the time was spent in the club car where my companions engaged in lively, and at times heated, conversation. Most of my association the past two years had been with academic people, so it was refreshing to listen to another slice of the public. No one paid much attention to me, a humble government employee, and, since I stuck to Coca Cola, I was not included in their drinking rounds.

Hitler had just marched into Czechoslovakia in March 1939, which they strongly opposed. About what should be done about it, there was considerable controversy. Two of the party felt we should build up our army, the same way as we had our navy the year before (with an appropriation of one billion dollars). The other three felt that an army increase would only invite trouble, since FDR would use the build-up to embroil us in the European mess. But they all supported the new neutrality act, which allows the shipment of arms to Britain on a cash and carry basis on British ships. The old neutrality act prohibited sale of arms to both combatants, (although everyone knew that weapons were being shipped to Britain through Canada).

The conversation dragged on past midnight, with no effort being made to move us out of the club car. By the time I went to my berth, I had drunk so much Coke that my hands trembled when I made the entry into my notebook.

May 27, 1939

Early morning the train pulled into Union Station in Washington. I watched the trunk being off-loaded and brought into the baggage room. Despite the early hour, crowds of people thronged the station, most in business suits, some in uniform and a few in those strange zoot suits, which I saw for the first time. The woman seated behind the information desk assured me that the hotels were completely booked up. Moreover, the Army and Navy Club was also a full, the "Y" was closed for the month and the closest available accommodations were outside the city.

I remembered that Fort Myers was close by, just across the Potomac River. After standing in line for 20 minutes at the taxi ramp, I finally secured a taxi and swung my valise inside. As we crossed the Potomac River on the way to the military post, I noticed a huge building under construction. The driver told me it was the new Army headquarters and that it was supposed to be the largest office building in the world.

We soon reached old Fort Myers. I showed my orders to the sentry, and the driver took me to the Bachelor Officers' Quarters and waited for the outcome.

Inside, a grey-haired black private was seated at the duty desk. He was in complete uniform, despite the heat, with freshly polished shoes and shiny buttons. He jumped up and asked if he could be of help. I explained my predicament: that I was here in Washington to report to the Army Headquarters and needed a bed.

He examined the orders carefully, only he held the page upside-down. He asked my rank, which he should have known from the orders, and told me that he had nothing left for company rank, but he did have one room for majors and above. and offered to put me up there until some senior officer showed up to claim it.

Welcome news. I dismissed the driver waiting outside.

The private grabbed my valise and led me to my room in an adjacent building, on the way pointing out the nearby shower room and the towel closet. Quickly, I undressed and showered, trailing water on the floor on the way back to my room. After donning my uniform, I returned to the private and asked that he call a taxi to take me to the Army Department. It turned out that the Army runs a station wagon to the Army building every 20 minutes.

I was dropped off at a somber, gray stone building. A crowd of men in uniform, mostly officers, hung around the front entrance. Inside, the hallways were jammed with offices, most seeking a change of orders.

Personnel were on the second floor. Since the elevator was reserved for field officers, I walked up the stairs, or tried to, but there was a long line of officers waiting to enter the personnel office. After a 15-minute wait, I approached a tired warrant officer and showed him my orders. He, in turn, led me to a lieutenant colonel, who read my orders and studied me carefully. After pronouncing my name, he glanced at a memo and informed me that I was to report to the office of the chief-of-staff at 0930 tomorrow. I was to have in my possession a military passport. The warrant officer explained that I could have the photos taken in the basement of this building, and gave me directions to the passport office nearby.

Military passport! Service overseas! That usually means Panama or the Philippines!

After waiting an hour for the photos, I walked over to the nearby passport office. It was a unimpressive one-story, white, clapboard building on the grounds of the State Department. A tough gray-haired lady sat well entrenched behind a high marble counter, directly opposite the entrance. I informed her of my needs and she handed me an application, which I filled out and returned to her, together with the two photos.

She examined the application, then attached the photos with a paper clip and told me to come back the day after tomorrow for the military passport! I tried to explain that my orders stated that I was to appear before them tomorrow, with the military passport. It was like talking to the proverbial marble statue. Twenty years of Washington bureaucracy had left her bereft of human understanding. As I retreated toward the exit, the thought came to me that I had once met a graduate student named Lois at a party. In the course of our conversation, Lois told us that her mother was in charge of the passport office in Washington.

But that was five years ago. Was the mother still here? What was Lois surname? Lois what? Lois what? It came to me as I was about to leave. Lois Greene! I did an about face and return to the counter. I asked if I could see Mrs. Greene and explained that I knew her daughter, Lois.

Miss Sour Puss told me to wait and disappeared down the hall. Five minutes later she returned and announced that I could pick up the passport in 3 hours.

Hallelujah! I forewent lunch and hung around the passport office until the military passport was handed to me. After, I walked back to the Army Building and caught a ride to Fort Myers. The sweat was pouring down my body, so I showered and changed into a pair of slacks and sport shirt and went outside for a stroll. Not too smart walking around with the temperature in the nineties, but better than remaining in a room without air conditioning and with a rusted fan, wondering what was coming next.

Halfway down the track around the parade grounds, I saw three strange vehicles parked at the upper end of the drill field. They were heavily armored and might have resembled tanks without their cannons and without tracks. The smallest of the vehicles, the strangest of all, looked like a midget's conveyance.

Two mechanics were fiddling with the wheels. I approached the younger, an alert young fellow in his late twenties, who was oiling some bearings, and when he looked up, I asked politely what kind of vehicle these were.

He told me that they were Christie tanks, the M-1929, the M-1931 and the "Airborne Smasher," designed to be carried by an airplane.

He went on to say that his father, John Walter Christie, was the inventor of the Christie tanks. The front armor is slanted to deflect an incoming round, and the tanks has shock absorbers on every wheel. About the hole in the turret, he explained that the cannon had been left out, so that the Army could choose whatever caliber they wanted, up to 75mm. This astounded me, since I hadn't known that a tank could be fitted with a 75mm gun. When I pointed out that the tanks had no tracks, he assured me that they didn't need tracks for this terrain and that the tracks could be easily installed before moving across country.

Would I like a ride? You bet I would! I climbed in beside him into the turret. It was ghastly hot inside, and my arm burned whenever it touched the metal. We started off slowly around the track and then speeded up, but the speed was limited by the sharp turns. Even so, I estimated that we were traveling more than 50 miles/hr! He then took the tank across the drill field, so that I could get a feeling for the suspension. Smoother than a truck, I told him, and he seemed pleased to hear it. After the ride, I headed for the BOQ, and returned with an armful of Cokes for Christie, Jr., and the mechanic, who were lounging in the shade of the M-1931 tank.

Down the field we caught a glimpse of an older white-haired man, rushing toward us. Mr. Christie was back, furious at the reception he had received from Army procurement. He announced that they were leaving immediately.

As an aside, the son whispered that his father had not expected the Army to accept delivery and that Christie had come mainly to get a release from procurement, so that he could sell the tanks to the Soviets and the plans to Poland and Great Britain, all of whom were anxious to incorporate Christie's ideas into their own tank programs.

The old man ordered his helpers to fetch the two huge Christie flatbed trucks. Soon, the three tanks were loaded onto the trucks, and off they went, leaving me with the empty Coke bottles.

The whole encounter had been something of an eye opener for me. At the Academy we had been taught that the tank was designed primarily to support an infantry advance. Also, that future prospects for the tanks were poor, since the advent of the huge anti-tank guns, which can easily halt any tank advance. Accordingly, tank development in the American Army had been passed through a succession of unsympathetic patrons, until it finally came under the control of the cavalry board, where it is now. Imagine! Entrusting the fate of the tanks to horsemen!

May 28, 1939

I presented myself in uniform with Sam Brown belt at the stated time at the crowded headquarters of the Deputy Chief of War Plans at the War Department building and was directed to a small office of a Brigadier General Brooks F. Moore, according to the nameplate. Also seated in the office, was a tall, mustached gentleman, impeccably dressed in a well-tailored suit. I saluted General Moore and announced that I was reporting as directed.

Salute returned. He nodded at the seated figure and introduced him as a Mr. McHenry of the State Department. No first name, no title. They were here, he told me, to discuss my prospective assignment.

After emptying the contents of my official file onto his desk, he proceeded to examine each paper, handing it afterwards to the seated gentleman, who put on a pair of glasses to study them.

He ran through the list. Graduated 15th in his class at the Academy; two years in the Canal Zone; two years with the Civilian Conservation Corps; two years ROTC at South Indiana State; date of promotions; efficiency reports; Captain (Temporary).

Next, my family history. Running synopsis (no dates). Father: Charles Manning. Born Nauhut, Germany. Graduated high school (gymnasium). Worked his way to U.S. as a galley hand; scholarship student at MIT; Degree (Chemical Engineering); Founded Manning Industries, bought by DuPont after his death. He further scanned the papers and mumbled as he handed them off. Served as Second Assistant Deputy Chief of War Industries in Washington during the late war; economic advisor to two presidents. Subject now deceased.

Next, my mother, *nee* Juliette De Chevny-Running. Synopsis. Born Lorraine, Germany, the daughter of Paula De Chevny, the pianist. Met husband during a concert tour in the States. Married in Massachusetts. One child. Subject now deceased.

When asked about the foreign languages spoken in our home, I told them I spoke French with my mother, German with my father and German when we were all together. I could have added that I spoke Lotharingian (a country dialect), with my nurse, but I let it pass.

Mr. McHenry asked me a few questions in perfect high German and seemed satisfied with my answers. General Moore then looked at McHenry, who nodded. It was then that the general told me that they were considering sending me to Berlin as a military attaché and asked if there was any reason why I would be unfit for overseas service.

None, I told them. Service Overseas? Privately, I had hoped for a newly formed infantry company. The newspapers have been talking about re-starting conscription and the need for qualified officers to train the incoming draftees.

The Brigadier General went on to explain that the president had recalled our ambassador in Berlin after the Crystal Night in 1938 when the Nazis broke the windows of the Jewish shops and burned the synagogues. Now we have only a *charge d'affaires* in Berlin and that limits our access to official functions.

He further explained that my predecessor had been run out of the country for indiscrete behavior and asked me whether I could be trusted to toe the line.

I assured him that I could be trusted. He instructed me to wait outside for five minutes and then to come back in without knocking. Five minutes flew by in an instant, and I walked back in.

They had found my qualifications acceptable. I was now a military attaché. They'll be two of us, but I'll be mostly by myself. The General reached for his phone and, after discussing me with someone, instructed me to speak to the warrant officer in personnel, who would cut my orders and arrange transportation.

I saluted and walked out.

The warrant officer spent almost an hour with me, drawing up orders and arranging transportation. Steamship tickets had been sold out on the British liners because of the impending coronation, so I was given passage on a German ship: a second-class ticket, since third class had already been filled. And as for per diem expenses, I was told to keep a strict accounting of the *en route* expenditures and hand them in to the next paymaster.

After returning to Fort Myers, I found myself with time on my hands, so I walked over to the commanding general 's office and asked one of the older civilian secretaries whether Fort Myers had a reading program for illiterate soldiers.

She immediately broke into a laugh, then excused herself, saying that the Red Cross lady was at this very moment in the building, trying to set up a program for illiterates and recommended I speak with her. The Red Cross lady was seated in her office on the second floor. After explaining to her the predicament of one of the BOQ privates, she promised to look into it.

After, I walked to the Officers Club, which was just opening, and placed a call to Mr. Desmond Everett White, the director of the Manning Trust Fund, whom I had promised to keep informed of my whereabouts. He was interested to learn of my new station and instructed me without fail to look up Christopher Weisbart, his old and dear friend and director of the German Commercial Bank, who could be trusted to look after my financial needs. I assured him that I would, but doubted that my financial needs would be great.

May 31, 1939

Before dawn, I left the BOQ dressed in civvies, and caught the first ride to the train station. After purchasing my ticket at the military window, I showed it to the baggage clerk, who assured me that the trunk would be on my train. The trip to New York was uncomfortable, the car dirty, and it took more than the usual 4 hours before reaching Pennsylvania station. The trunk was off-loaded, and I looked for some way to transport it to Pier 91, where my ship, the Hanover, was docked. A taxi was out of the question because of the size of the trunk.

Just then a horse and wagon rolled by the station. It looked empty, so I flagged down the driver. He was more than willing to take me to the pier and, with the kind assistance of the baggage men, we loaded up the wagon. Clip, clop off we went in majestic style past Macy's and Gimbels on 34th street. We stopped near Eighth Avenue, long enough for me to dash into a men's haberdashery to make a few purchases for the trip, and the salesman made the fastest sale in his life. Down to the river we went, and up to the pier, passing a long line of taxis waiting to discharge their passengers. I found some stevedores who unloaded the trunk and brought it into a large hall, all decked out with swastikas—the first I had ever seen in real life. Before Indiana, I had been out in Utah.

The American customs stamped my military passport without so much as a glance. Then I got on the end of a line of passengers waiting to be processed by the steamship company. After 20 minutes, my turn came. They inspected my passport and my ticket and had me fill out a questionnaire. I was handed tags to fix to my trunk and valise and was assured that both would be brought to my stateroom. The formalities concluded, I drifted out onto the pier. There it was, the *Hanover*, flying the swastika. The crowd of passengers waiting to board slowly grew larger. Standing off by himself, I saw a rather husky young man with a somewhat familiar face, whom I recognized as belonging to a Yale All-American football player whom I had seen in the newsreels playing in an Army–Yale game. The sports writers loved him. What was his name? Lloyd Sutton.

We struck up a conversation. Sure enough, it was the football player, now graduated. Instead of joining his father's well-known soap company where he could spend the day frolicking at the local country club, he enrolled at Georgetown for a master's degree; passed the foreign service exam and was now a vice-consul on the way to Dundee, Scotland traveling on a standard third-class ticket (for vice-consuls).

Standing around gabbing made us hungry. There was no food service on the pier, so we persuaded the guard to let us back into the hall, where we could get some hot dogs from the vendor's cart outside the building. A few sauerkraut-dogs and a Coke later, we crept back onto the pier.

Boarding had just begun for first class. I invited Lloyd to join me this evening for dinner, but he replied that the ship does not allow third class to come up to the second-class deck, but we could meet tomorrow in the gym, which serves all three classes

The call went out for second-class passengers. I went up the gangway and was greeted by a four-striper and a three-striper, both gushing a mechanical "velcome aboard"; and then by a two-striper purser who examined my ticket and checked my name off his list. He informed me, in English, that I would have my stateroom all to myself, since the Hanover knows how to treat an American officer. I thanked him for what appeared to be a courtesy. Further, he was seating me in the first-class dining room. When I protested that I had no tuxedo, he informed me that a dark suit would do nicely. I actually do have a tuxedo in my trunk, I thought.

My cabin was a well-maintained stateroom with two beds and a small window that looked out on some lifeboats. Meanwhile, my trunk and valise had arrived. According to the steward who came around, the captain would be conducting a boat drill as soon as we left the pier, so I took off my shoes, lay down on the bed and promptly fell asleep.

Clang! Clang! went the fire bell. I quickly donned my kapok life jacket and hurried to my boat station. The Statue of Liberty appeared majestically off the starboard side, and the passengers abruptly interrupted their babbling to stare at it. A thrill passed up and down my spine. Even the crew who tried to show indifference could not refrain from interrupting their work to glance at her as we sailed by.

The drill over, I returned to my stateroom, showered, set the alarm and promptly went back to sleep until the dinner gong woke me up.

Dressed in a dark suit, I stood out from the formally dressed men in the first-class dining room. The *maitre d'* led me to my assigned table and sat me down opposite a young lady in her early twenties. I now understood why I was placed in the first-class dining.

We introduced ourselves: one couple from Maine (boat builder), the second from Pittsburgh (steel) and the parents of the girl from New York (broadcasting). When they asked me what I did for a living, I told them. The boat builder promptly informed me that he had been a first lieutenant with the AEF during the second battle of the Marne, and that he had little respect for the regular Army ("excuse me for saying that"). And when the good people saw that I did not drink alcohol, I was summarily dismissed as peculiar.

They chattered incessantly about their forthcoming stay in London, the coronation and the social events. The girl sat sullen and indifferent and resisted any attempt to draw her into the conversation. No one paid attention to me, until the end of the dinner when the waiter reached for my plate.

I told him to leave it, since I hadn't finished. Only I said it in German. This aroused their curiosity, and I had to further explain that I was on my way to the Berlin Embassy, whereupon I was re-classified as your typical scrounger.

The meal over, the music began, and in accordance with my social obligations (well stressed at the Academy), I invited Cornelia to dance. Somewhat reluctantly, she followed me to the small dance floor.

She begged forgiveness for her rudeness and explained that she had lost patience listening to the garbage. She had just graduated from Vassar College and had a good chance of getting a job as junior copy editor at *Time* magazine, but instead, her parents insisted that she come along on this trip to Britain.

Despite my first impression, Cornelia was a charming girl: tall, handsome, fair-haired, blue-eyed with an athlete's body (tennis), just the right person for a friend I know. I described him and suggested that she meet him, but since he was travelling third class, she could only see him in the gym, where he would be in the morning. She seemed interested and promised to look him up.

Back at the table, I concluded my social obligation by inviting the other women to dance. They refused. We listened for a half hour to the men dissecting FDR, after which, I said my goodnights and took my leave.

June 1, 1939

I rose early, had a solitary breakfast, then changed into my gym clothes. As I entered the gym, I noticed Cornelia and Lloyd in deep conversation. I waved to them before drifting over to the exercise machines. An hour later they were still talking and hardly noticed me when I left.

My plan was to use this trip as an opportunity to learn German geography and customs. The second-class library was luxuriously paneled, and the shelves held a large collection of books in English and German.

I explained my needs in German to a young, fair-haired librarian wearing a uniform with one stripe, seated at a small desk facing the entrance. She led me into the appropriate section, and I selected a 10-year-old German volume which I took to the library table and began reading. Initially, the gothic script was a nuisance, since my knowledge was chiefly in the spoken language, but I soon overcame that obstacle.

And so, the time passed. At 10.30, I caught a glimpse of the purser coming into the library and whispering to the librarian. She turned her head to glance at me. After handing her a paper, he departed. What was that about, I wondered?

I resolved to skip lunch and continue reading. About 12:00 the librarian came up to me and said, in German, that she had to close for an hour but would be open after that. As I got up to go, she told me her name was Hilde and asked if I would like to see the crew's quarters. Since I had an awesome interest in naval architecture, I followed her down a flight of stairs and along the passageways. She was well-built, which even the uniform could not conceal, with dark hair and a well-rounded derriere which swayed enticingly as I followed behind.

Her cabin was a small compartment, with two stacked berths. After very scant preliminaries, we found ourselves entangled in the lower bunk for a busy half hour. The embrace over, we lounged in the sack to catch our breath; whereupon she commented that she knew nothing about me and proceeded to question me as to where I was born, where I went to school, the year I graduated from the Academy, the names of my parents, etc. I answered her until the questions became tiring, whereupon she leapt out of bed and dashed into the bathroom. She emerged saying that she had to run and rushed out of the stateroom.

After a hasty shower, I vacated the stateroom, and returned to the library. Hilde had been replaced by an older woman with a sharp nose and thin lips. My book still lay on the library table, and I resumed reading.

At dinner, Cornelia had not shown up, and her parents were disturbed. They asked me if I had seen her, and I told them not since this morning at the gym. The meal began. The waiter asked me in German whether he should serve the girl soup, but I advised him to wait

Halfway through the first course, Cornelia made an appearance in a hastily chosen skirt and blouse, with her hair somewhat disarranged. She apologized for being late and said that she had just lost track of the time.

The meal resumed, with the parents trying to conceal their embarrassment. When the music began, Cornelia gladly accepted my dance invitation. She told me that I was right and that she was so thankful I told her about Lloyd. I suggested that if she planned to see him again, to make sure that she was back on time. Her parents were about ready to search the ship.

June 2, 1939

Morning like yesterday. Cornelia and Lloyd were huddled together in a corner of the gym, oblivious to the march of civilization around them.

In the library, Hilde was back at her desk. I opened my book and resumed reading. The same thing happened. The library closed at 12, and Hilde and I went to her cabin. After, as we lay in her rack, she continued her questions. Nothing vital–no military secrets, only personal questions with special emphasis on dates. Again, when she finished with me, she flew out of the cabin.

At dinner, Cornelia was there at the table on time with a radiant smile that proclaimed joy to the world. The political discussion among the men continued, as they appraised the prospects of Robert A. Taft, a Republican war horse and a prospective challenger to FDR.

Cornelia was beaming on the dance floor and whispered to me that she was in love.

I can hardly wait to hear what her parents will say when she tells them that she's fallen for the vice-consul in Dundee, Scotland!

June 3, 1939

Much the same as yesterday. At noontime, I passed up a visit to the crew's quarters, explaining that I had promised to meet a friend in the gym. Instead, I had an afternoon nap. Evening, Cornelia was all aglow and led the conversation, while her parents looked on suspiciously.

June 4, 1939

Same routine. Reading, and then a visit to Hilde's cabin. Only the questions became incessant, far more than the product of casual curiosity. When I indicated my displeasure, she broke off and left.

While dressing, I noticed a paper lying face down under the glass cover of her make-up table, which I fished out and examined. Stapled to the paper was my photo, taken as I came up the gangway. The paper contained a full page of questions and beside each was a space for a handwritten response: where I was born, name of my secondary school, date of graduation, etc. etc. etc.

The incessant questioning was now explained. A few spaces were still vacant, so I filled them in myself with a fountain pen lying on the table. After making a few bold-faced corrections, I replaced the paper back under the glass.

The evening meal was the last for Cornelia and the three couples who were leaving early tomorrow when the ship docked at Southampton. The kitchen tried to put an extra effort into the last meal, but by now the men passengers had grown tired of the chewy, range-fed Argentina beef, and scorned the chef's efforts.

Cornelia was aglow when we danced together. She confided that she was going up to Dundee with Lloyd and asked if there were any jobs at the consulate for an American citizen. I confessed my ignorance but pointed out that she risked being turned down for employment everywhere in Dundee. Job or no job she insisted that she was going.

After saying my goodbyes to the people at the table, I walked out. At the door, the *maitre d'* drew me aside and begged me to return for the farewell party. He pleaded so forcefully that I found it hard to refuse him.

Reluctantly, I returned to the table. The diners all wore paper hats, blew toy horns and waved finger clappers. The women had brightly colored leys around their necks. But there was no joy in Mudville. Cornelia had left, and Daddy was livid with rage.

With a most belligerent look, he accused me of introducing his daughter to a money chaser. I told him that whatever he thinks of Lloyd that he was no money chaser. His father was Reginald Sutton, who could match him 10-to-1, for every dollar that he has in the bank.

This cooled him down a bit. We ate the cherry cake and watched the waiters put on a show.

June 5, 1939

Next morning, I heard the commotion as the ship docked at Southhampton, but remained in bed until the passengers had departed. Hilde was in the library, but did not talk to me, and after lunch, her sharp-nosed replacement took over. By then, I had finished the book and had learned a great deal about German geography and customs.

At dinner, I was moved to a new table, this one in the second-class dining room, where the passengers were all German-speaking. All seemed well off, and all were enthusiastic supporters of the Nazi party.

June 6, 1939

We docked at dawn in Hamburg. The pier was decked with huge Nazi banners, and the band played martial music. I had made arrangements to have my trunk sent to the appropriate Station in Berlin, but took my valise with me. The purser himself brought me to the German customs, who stamped my passport and chalked my baggage. The purser acknowledged my thanks with an arm's length *Heil Hitler* salute. Aboard ship, I had seen and heard the greeting, but it had never been directed at me.

At the nearby railroad station, I changed some money and bought a second-class roomette to Berlin. First class, I was told, had been cancelled indefinitely. The room turned out to be very small, barely large enough to swing the proverbial cat, and that was before the bed was pulled down. Initially the countryside we passed was rather flat and uninteresting, not unlike a train ride through parts of Ohio. Instead of dressing for the dining car, I had sandwiches brought in, but the bread turned out to be stale. Later in the day, the scenery became more interesting, but by then dusk had fallen, and I had the sleeping car attendant prepare my bed.

June 6, 1939

We arrived early at the Berlin railroad station. The building was jammed with crowds of people, some in working clothing; many, including the youngsters, in uniform. Huge swastika banners hung down the walls of the station, giving color to what would otherwise be drab interiors. At the taxi ramp, I was informed that taxis were only for those on army or party business or pregnant women in labor. Lugging my large valise onto a trolley or underground railway car had no appeal for me, so I approached the taxi checker, who was supervising the taxi queue, and showed him my military passport. He allowed me back in line. The taxi brought me into the center of Berlin to the old Paris Plaza, where the driver pointed out the Adlon Hotel, the Ministry of Propaganda building and next to it, the old Bluecher Palace, which now serves as the new American Embassy.

A long line of people had formed outside the left corner of the building facing Hermann Goering Street (new name), and next to it, a somewhat smaller line, composed of what sounded through the open taxi window like impatient Americans. The driver drove around both lines and brought me to the main gate. A Marine challenged us, but let us through as soon as I flashed my identification.

Off to the right of the building on a small plot of grass, a small Marine detachment had just finished flag-raising and was undergoing inspection. An officer passed slowly down the line, carefully examining haircuts, uniforms, etc. The inspection over, I approached him.

Captain Dwaine Mosby was his name, and he commanded the small Marine detachment. He was of medium build, square-jawed and somewhat older than me, but lean and muscular in a way I would prefer not to encounter in a hostile engagement.

I asked about the people lined up on the side of the building. He shook his head sadly and told me that the small line were Americans residing in Germany who wanted to leave Germany immediately. War fears. The second line were mostly German Jews, trying to obtain visas for the United States, even though the quotas had already been filled. He told me that I may be asked to interview some of them, if the consular staff were to fall behind in their work.

The main entrance led into a large reception hall with a marble floor and gold-trimmed fixtures. On the floor below were the canteen for the staff and sleeping quarters for the Marines.

We left my valise near the entrance, but I took my ancient briefcase with my orders. Captain Moby brought me up the stairs to the embassy offices and senior living quarters. The largest apartment was now vacant, since the ambassador's recall. Next to it, were the quarters of Duncan Bradford, the Consul General, now in charge (*charge d'affaires*), and his wife, Kirstin. Kirstin Bradford had been an anthropology professor at the University of Chicago and is now on the visiting faculty at Humboldt University in Berlin.

Mosby's apartment was next to the Bradshaw quarters, and he invited me in for breakfast. The apartment had a large immaculate parlor, a small dining room, a kitchen and bedrooms in the back. There was also one room with a posted "Keep Out" sign, which he did not bother to identify. His wife and son joined us. Eugenia is a slender somewhat retiring fair-haired woman in her early thirties; the boy, Clayton, a twelve-year-old charmer: with a merry sense of humor. The father explained that the boy attended Mrs. Robinson's school for diplomatic children, now in recess. Mrs. Robinson was a hard taskmaster, since her students upon graduation must be prepared to take either the baccalaureate (France), the arbiter (Germany) or the College Entrance (US).

We sat down to a pancake breakfast with maple syrup (molasses). Duncan went on to discuss with me what I had already heard: the embassy was somewhat isolated since the recall of our ambassador; I must, at all times, avoid becoming embroiled in any public controversy, no matter the provocation. My predecessor, he explained, had gotten into a fight with some storm troopers who were beating up an old Jew, and he was summarily ordered out of the country.

The Mosbys had been in Berlin for seven years, which was a surprise to me, since the Marine detachment was so small, and seven years is a long time for a Marine officer to remain at one station. A Marine officer, I might add, who spoke perfect German, as did his son. I also detected a slight accent in Eugenia's English, and Mosby explained that Eugenia and her sister Kirstin, had both been born in Germany but had left early in life.

The breakfast over, I was taken to the quarters of Duncan Bradford, our Consul General and *charge d'affaires*, who verified my orders. A tall, distinguished man in his early forties, he was clearly a State Department prototype. Introductions were exchanged, and his scholarly-looking wife, Kirstin, joined us. She looked slightly younger than her husband, a handsome woman with grayish hair, black spectacles and a pencil sticking out of her braided tresses.

Bradford insisted that I have another cup of coffee—American coffee, imported from Denmark without the need for ration cards. A servant girl brought in the coffee pot and poured me another cup. Bradford went over again what Mosby had already told me. My chief job was to stay out of trouble.

The coffee-break over, Mosby continued the tour. He pointed to the secured communications room nearby, which only he and Mr. Bradford are permitted to enter, apart from the men who

work there, who wear holsters when they come
on duty. Down the hall was the office of the
military attachés. He unlocked the door and
handed me the key. The room seemed to have
been unoccupied for a long time. In it were two
ugly metal desks, two desk chairs, a few empty
file cabinets, unattractive overhead bulbs, a
partially blacked-out window looking out to
Paris Square and an inch of dust everywhere.
Mosby promised to have the office cleaned up.

The naval attaché, he explained, had moved to
Wilhelmshaven, to be near the German naval
command. The air attaché, Major Charles Fox,
was following the entourage of Hermann
Goering. His was a remarkable story. He had
been a flier in the Great War, whose squadron,
in the closing months of the war, had engaged
in combat the Red Circus squadron formerly
led by the Red Baron and subsequently led by
Hermann Goering, who had succeeded Freiherr
Manfred von Richthofen after his death. When
Major Fox had come to Berlin, Goering learned
of his background and has lionized him ever
since. Fox is invited to all the Goering
banquets, introduced to all the Luftwaffe
generals and invited to accompany Goering on

his inspection tours of the aircraft factories. Of course, the main purpose is to impress Fox with German Air supremacy, just as Goering impressed Charles Lindbergh, but Charlie Fox is as sly as his name implies, and well able to detect when the inspection tours had returned to the same factory by another entrance in order to inflate the estimates of the numbers of airplanes being manufactured. Fox reports twice a year in person to General Henry "Hap" Arnold, the Army Air Force Chief.

By this time, the chief secretary, Helen, had arrived. She was a capable, rather pleasant looking woman in her late thirties, wearing a pleated skirt and jacket. Her really distinctive attribute was a pair of large breasts, which even the tight-fitting jacket could not conceal. She welcomed me and quickly rattled off the standing regulations, the embassy hours, payday schedules, etc. Application for my ration book has already been made through the German foreign office, and arrangements had been made for me to board at Mrs. (Ambassador) Marie Von Huzic's home. She runs the boarding house where my predecessors had stayed.

She cautioned me about the two chamber maids. If I were so unwise as to have a liaison with one of them, she would approach me after a month or so went by and tell me that she is pregnant and that she needs a gold coin to go home and have the matter attended to.

I resolved to heed her advice. As to where I would take my meals, Helen informed me that whether at the boarding house or at the casino, with the Marines and most of the embassy personnel, that either would require that I turn in my ration book. Most newcomers take their meals at the embassy.

I told her I would take them at the canteen.

Mosby brought me over to the consular section on the right side of the building and introduced me to the personnel. The line of visa applicants went out the door into the street. Despondent people of all ages crowded the rooms. Women cried; babies wailed; men sobbed, hopelessness shown on their faces.

Since this was my first day, Mosby arranged to have me taken by embassy limousine to my new home. He introduced me to Vincent, the

official chauffer, who took my valise and off
we went.

Vincent pointed out the streetcar which would
ordinarily take me to and from the embassy to
my home. He tried to explain the subway and
the elevated systems, but I resolved to remain
with the streetcar for the time being. We came
to the residence on Kant Street, a large,
respectable home in the Charlottenburg section
of the city. A photo of Adolph Hitler hung on
the wall of the entrance hall. The major domo,
Klaus, greeted me and promised to have my
trunk fetched. He introduced me to the owner, a
Mrs.(Ambassador) Augustina Von Huzic,
whose late husband had been an ambassador for
Kaiser Wilhelm the Second. I was invited to
dine with her tonight as her guest, even though
I had told Klaus that I would take my meals in
the embassy.

My room was on the first (European second)
floor. Somber and dark with one blacked-out
window, it had a huge bed with thick feather
quilts and an embroidered pillow. Instead of
closets, there was a large, dark mahogany
wardrobe, which crowded the room and seemed

to squeeze out the air. The chambermaids appeared, and Klaus made the introductions. Buxom was their best description, with their salient features poorly concealed under the maids' uniforms.

As the girls tidied up the room, there was a lot of bending over, pulling down aprons and brushing up against me as they passed by. Meanwhile the trunk had arrived and the two girls, Trudy and Heidi, helped me unpack.

The first thing they saw was the picture of Cynthia, my former fiancée. They picked up the picture and examined it keenly and asked if she was a movie star. I replied that she was my fiancée and that she was coming soon. After that, their assault lessened, and I gratefully set the picture on my bedside table.

At 8 pm, dressed in a dark suit, I presented myself in the dining room. There were lengthy introductions to each of the other six boarders. One was from Slovakia, another a Swedish fish salesman, and the rest from the different embassies. We spoke in German, with Frau (Ambassador) von Huzic at the head of the table. The conversation was as vapid as the food was ordinary, but at least the service was rather good, I thought.

After the obligatory post-prandial German cognac, which I scarcely touched, (except to press the glass to my lips whenever our hostess toasted Kaiser Wilhelm II), I made my way back to my room. The toilette was down the hall; the bath next to it, but we were obliged to give Klaus 5 hours' notice to ensure that the furnace was properly stoked. I crawled into bed and immediately sunk down into the mattress, as if mired in quicksand. A wedge had been placed behind the pillow, with the expectation that I would sleep sitting up. I promptly removed the wedge and drifted off to slumber land.

June 7, 1939

I left the house early, taking with me my valise containing toilette articles, towels, and a change of clothing, so that I could shower in the ambassador's quarters. The trolley had another car attached to it, both with clean but well-worn interiors. It stopped a few blocks from my destination, and, valise in hand, I had to make my way on foot.

After showering, I had my breakfast in the canteen. I found myself seated with several consular officers who were complaining about the hectic interviews. One of them made some oblique comments about Mosby: his concern for the applicants was going to get us all kicked out of Germany. I did not quite understand the remark, other than assume that that Mosby had a deep concern for those applicants.

Helen had not yet arrived, but on her desk was a stack of the *Berlin Zeitung*, the *Voelkischer Beobachter* and the *Paris Herald Tribune*. I helped myself to one of each and brought them back to my office (which had been dusted). The *Herald Tribune* mentioned that the bill to introduce the draft was working its way through Congress and was meeting with stiff opposition. The Berlin newspapers spoke of the growing crisis in Poland and the persecution of the German people in Danzig, which is an internationalized city between Germany and East Prussia. There was also mention of various troop movements and changes in the German command, but without a table of organization I could not understand what was being reported.

Helen came in, and I handed back the newspapers, neatly folded. Since she was unsure when my pay would commence, I decided to follow Desmond Everett White's advice and pay a visit to Dr. Christopher Weisbart, the director of the German Commercial Bank. A double-decker bus took me there. The bank, a stately grey stone structure, was situated just off the busy Kuerfurstendamm on Leibniz Street. A pre-World War structure most likely.

Breezing past the ancient uniformed guard at the front door, I asked a teller to direct me to Dr. Weisbart and handed her my card. A few minutes later a gray-haired secretary came rushing up to me and escorted me in the brass bird-cage elevator up one floor to the director's office. Director Dr. Weisbart himself ushered me in. He was a rugged man in his early forties, with a pleasant smile and a hearty handshake. He greeted me in German and mentioned that Desmond telephoned that I would be arriving. He explained that he had already set up a checking account (and at this point switched to English), and recommended that I keep no more than $5,000 on deposit. Money can always be brought in, but it was sometimes difficult to take out. Back in German, he said that if I needed to write a larger check, I could make it out to the National Bank Trust of Boston, whose checkbook I had, and the check would be honored.

There were some papers to sign, but the whole meeting took no more than a half hour. Director Dr. Christopher Weisbart, it appeared, is a good friend of Mr. White and had stayed with him on two occasions at his summer home on Martha's Vineyard. I left with the impression that this man could be trusted.

June 8, 1939

Decided to spend the day sightseeing and walking through the city. Berlin is like no other city in the world. For one thing, it appears to be completely immersed in war preparations. Signs abounded, directing pedestrians to air raid shelters. Sandbags were everywhere, propped up against buildings. Military vehicles which I could not yet identify crowded the streets, together with a large number of big (*grosse*) Mercedes, which I am told, belong to party members or rich people on the right side of the Nazis. A few reminders of the savage Crystal Night rampage were still evident, with the faded "Out Jew" graffiti on the walls, but most of that had been removed.

I took a double-decker bus along the Unter den Linden Boulevard and walked along Friedrich and Potsdam Streets, trying to get some idea of current fashions. Men carrying red buckets would suddenly thrust the bucket at you and demand a donation for whatever was the cause of the day. When I walked into one of the fashionable shops that displayed something of interest in its window, I found the sales people were gone and that the manager himself waited on the customer. If you tell him you would like to see the item in the window, he tells you that it is on order, with an unknown date of delivery. Where other shops have customers lined up outside the store, you can be sure a shipment has arrived and will soon disappear. Many of the women office workers wear wooden clogs during the day, since new shoes are unobtainable; they reserve their leather shoes for evening wear. Those silk stockings still being worn usually have runs in them.

Those without runs suggest that the wearer has a boyfriend stationed in Paris.

Loudspeakers blast out marches, interspersed with announcements and news flashes from the DD (Dratloser Dienst) Radio Service. An occasional air raid alarm sends everyone scurrying for the nearest air raid shelter, while an officious warden herds the pedestrians down into a dark smelly basement. The drill over, the outdoor terraces quickly refill with laughing beer drinkers, and outwardly, the people seem confident of where there were being led.

The nightly blackout is strictly enforced. The headlights of the cars are masked, except for a small shaft of light. This, I am told, makes walking at night hazardous. When out after sundown, everyone is advised to wear some luminescent object. Some say that they can see the stars for the first time.

June 9, 1939

At the evening meal in the canteen, the chief of the Lost Passport Section, invited me to accompany him to one of the parties. There's always a party going on every night in the apartments of the embassy people, sometimes several parties. Tonight's party was in the home of three French embassy workers who were housed in an apartment building a few blocks from the French embassy, not far from the American embassy on Paris Place.

I bought a bottle of wine, selected from the well-stocked file cabinet of my consular friend, and off we went. A dozen couples were already in the apartment, and we entered without knocking. There were no formal introductions. Everyone seemed to know everyone else, or at least pretended to. Bottles were opened, drinks poured, drinking commenced, while the ancient gramophone valiantly belted out dance tunes, barely audible over the conversation. I was lucky enough to find in the kitchen a bottle of a horrible mineral water, called Radiumwasser Lauerberg. Refuse it, if ever served to you again!

A lithe French embassy secretary, Louisette, quickly identified me as a newcomer to the embassy scene and invited me to try out the dance floor, newly exposed from under the rolled-up carpet. During the dance, she clung to me so tightly, that I could feel the contour of every curve in her body. Between dances we talked and drank, she, the wine, and me, the Radiumwasser Lauerberg. There seemed no way to slow down her drinking, and the longer she drank, the merrier she got. She came from Rouen, France and before she took the job with the French embassy, she had worked in a law office, but the men there were etc., etc.

Meanwhile, a procession to the bedrooms began. If the couple lingered unnecessarily long, they were interrupted by a heavy knock on the door. All in good fun. Ha. Ha. Our turn came. I performed my obligated service, and we left the bedroom, our clothing carefully rearranged, before any knock sounded on the door. The drinking resumed, and I began to feel that I could not get Louisette home, though she lived in the same building two stories above this apartment. With difficulty, I got her into the elevator and then up two floors. After delivery, one of Louisette's roommates invited me in for a drink, but I begged off, promising to return another evening.

June 11, 1939

For five days now, I have been immersed in the nightly embassy circuit, and the time has come for me to withdraw. There must be more to living than this. The worst thing I saw was the widespread use of methamphetamines ("pervitin"), which they say is taken not only by the Wehrmacht but also by half of Berlin; and is readily available (or used to be) without prescription at the pharmacies. In addition, Helen warned me about associating with the foreign correspondents, expatriates or American outcasts. They hang around the bar at the Adlon. Once they get to know you, they tie up your telephone all day with requests for information or favors.

June 12, 1939

We were having coffee with Eugenia ("Jean") and Dwaine Mosby in their apartment, when the Cardenas family arrived with their little baby and its nursemaid. Morgan Swift Cardenas is a close friend of Jean Mosby, whom she visits almost daily. She is the daughter of the founder of the Swift Chocolate, and married shortly after graduation from

Wellesley College. She carries her one-year-old baby in a papoose bag in front of her, leaving one to wonder what the nursemaid is for. Her husband, Felix, the nephew of the former Mexican Minister of War, is a major in the Mexican Medical corps, a surgeon, and from all accounts, a superb surgeon, who works at the famous clinic of Professor Ernest Ferdinand Sauerbruch, the only foreign surgeon to have a regular appointment.

It goes without saying that Felix is of immense help to the American Embassy people, when it comes to referring them to the right party for medical attention; and so is highly regarded here.

From Felix, I learned that the military attachés will be meeting this evening. This information would ordinarily have been conveyed to me by the liaison officer of the German Foreign Office, who is also a reserve officer, but he had been called away by his regiment. Apparently, Mosby does not regularly attend the meetings, since he is not listed as a military attaché. Felix promised to call for me at 1900 (7:00 pm) at my lodging and bring me to the meeting, but he could not stay, since he will be on duty at the Charite Hospital. And, oh yes, I had to wear my uniform and all my ribbons and decorations.

Ribbons. All I had were two tiny ribbons: one from Panama, the other from Nicaragua. I don't even deserve the Nicaragua ribbon. My C.O. in Panama had asked me to hand-deliver a message to Nicaragua on the last day that the ribbon was authorized; and I had the gall to wear the ribbon. I also had a medal for marksmanship, given me at the Academy, but it was tiny and looked like something from a Boy Scout troop.

Felix called for me at my lodgings with his snappy little Mercedes, and we drove to the meeting place. It was in the back of a tavern called the Golden Hind. There were two dozen or so men dressed in civilian clothes standing in the room, and a long table in the rear, from where beer and wine were being served.

Felix introduced me to the gray-haired president of the mess, who had been conversing with his two companions. All three were of senior age, tall and thin with the prescribed thin military mustache. The president was a Spanish colonel, the two others, French and British officers of (I suspect) the same rank. All three wore beautifully tailored suits, but I could not help notice the heavily worn jacket of the Brit, Colonel Sir William Scott-Comfort. He, in turn, sized me up carefully, especially my ribbons, then smiled and bade me welcome to Berlin.

I was taken around the room to the other groups, and the same procedure was followed: introduction to the senior, and he, in turn, introduced me to the others in his group. The air attachés were off by themselves in a corner. As my apprehension lessened, I listened to what was being discussed. Everyone spoke German, and most were fluent; even the Brazilian and Portuguese attachés. Nevertheless, I could not quite follow the conversation when it dealt with German Army organization, i.e., which brigade was part of which division, etc. German units are often identified by the name of the commander rather than by a numerical designation, which can add to the confusion.

One thing I did notice. A heavy-set man, Yugoslavian I believe, was muttering something to a fair-haired officer who could only be Scandinavian, about the German mercy killing of 40,000 people for mental or physical deformity. The other attachés seem to be distancing themselves from the conversation. I listened but said nothing and vowed to ask Mosby about it.

June 13, 1939

Mittlekamp and Sons is one of the largest book-stores in Berlin, no more than a 15-minute walk from the embassy. I went to the military section in search for books about the German army. So far as I could see, most were biographies or autobiographies from the Great War. One book was featured, the autobiography of an infantry officer named Erwin Rommel, who was pictured on a small poster standing next to Adolph Hitler. The other books had nothing to do with a modern army, except for translations of the works of B.H.L. Hart and J.P. Fuller, two Englishmen who dealt with some early theories about tank warfare. I placed the English books and the Rommel autobiography in my shopping basket, but doubted that they would help me with my present needs.

Next to the military section were the European maps. These included a fine map of Germany with the new autobahn system; as well as four regional German maps. I selected two sets of all five maps, intending to send one set to the War Department, which in my experience, always lagged when it came to providing good contemporary maps. Most of what we got at the Academy were from the Civil War.

In passing through the otherwise well-stocked travel section, I could not help but notice that the Polish books were sold out, and in their place was a sign that said "on order." After, I visited the children's department on the upper floor. Little Clayton Mosby had a birthday coming up. I had in mind to get him *Kidnapped* by Robert Louis Stevenson, since Dwaine Mosby had told me that his son had adored *Treasure Island.* I found the *Kidnapped* book in German, and put it in my basket.

Still in the children's book department, I saw a life-sized cardboard cutout of a smiling boy in Hitler Youth uniform. Underneath was the device

Heckler and Wolf
Military information for the Hitler Youth

The publication consisted of 11 small, soft-cover booklets, each devoted to a different military subject: artillery, infantry, tanks, infantry, transportation, etc. Each page had numerous illustrations in color—beautiful color, better than those seen in American publications. Each gun, tank, armored car or airplane had the official designation, as well as the popular name; and besides each had a brief description, (e.g., the designation for an armored car: introduced 1931, speed 120 km/hr, seats six, etc.).

Children's books or not, they were just what I needed. I put two complete sets in my basket, with the one intended for the War Department. If they have difficulty with the German, they can always look at the pictures. The cashier's department separated my purchases into two packages and insisted on having the packages delivered to the Embassy, rather than allow me to carry them myself.

Helen arranged to have the one package sent to the Office of the Chief of Staff War Plans

Department. For my purposes, the *Heckler and Wolf* booklets were priceless, and I began to study them immediately.

June 18, 1939

After supper in the canteen, I resumed my studies. Later, Mosby interrupted my reading to invite me to his apartment for a cup of coffee. As we were chatting, his 1st/sergeant, dressed in civilian clothes, rushed into the apartment short of breath and clearly greatly disturbed.

It seems that the 1st/Sergeant and two of the men, all dressed in civvies, were at Muellers, a cabaret, minding their own business. Muellers is a noisy place, with brass band entertainment, walking distance from the embassy. Seated at a nearby table were two burly, brown-shirted SA men (Stormtroopers), making loud comments about foreigners, as if to provoke them. The 1st/sergeant thought it best to leave.

As they were walking out, one of the SA men shouted that they had not paid the bill! The manager ran up and tried to calm things down, but the SA men insisted that the police be called. Before they arrived, the sergeant managed to slip away to alert the captain.

Mosby and the 1st/Sergeant rushed off, and I followed behind them. An elderly policeman had meanwhile been summoned to the tavern, not overly happy at becoming involved. The manager, who knew Mosby from previous visits, told him what had happened.

Mosby shook his head in disbelief and explained that there must be some mistake. He went over to the table on which were two beer glasses and an empty *plat du jour*. After lifting the dish, he pulled out a 10-mark bill and ceremoniously handed it to the manager.

There was a faint scattering of applause from the other tables, and the SA men looked astounded. Mosby apologized to the policeman for the misunderstanding and led us back to the embassy. On the way back, the 1st/Sergeant insisted that they had left 10 marks on the table. Mosby expressed astonishment and winked to me.

June 21, 1939

Military attaché mess tonight, and I went in civilian clothes. Posted at the entrance to the back room was a notice inviting the military attachés to the military exercises of the Fourth Armored Brigade of the Schmidli Division on June 23rd. Without a table of organization, I could not quite orient myself, but I resolved to attend anyway.

I carried my usual glass of mineral water as I circulated, listening to the conversations, Some of it was by now intelligible, as when they discussed troop carriers or guns, but when it came to the different army units, I was lost. Clearly, I had bad need of a table of organization. The other attachés had them, but were in no rush to share one with me. From off to the side, I heard someone mention the Christie tank. My ears picked up. This was my opportunity!

"About the Christie tank, why, yes, I rode in the M-1931 Christie tank and inspected the M-1929. Quiet. Quite interesting, but my job right now is to get hold of a table of organization."

My little interjection had been heard by many, and word quickly spread around the room. A few minutes later the British officer, Colonel Sir William Scott-Comfort, approached me. He walked with a noticeable limp from a war injury. In a quiet voice, he asked that I say nothing about the Christie tank.

With that, he hobbled away. My first impulse was to ignore him. What right had he to tell me what to do? But better instincts prevailed. Here is a badly wounded professional soldier, probably in reduced financial straits, making a request of me, on behalf of a government whom we were supporting.

So, I left early, to avoid further discussions. Not that I knew much about the Christie. In fact, nothing. My talk had been all bluff. On the way back to my lodging, I recalled that Christie's son had said something about selling the plans to Britain and the Poles, which might have been why Colonel Scott-Comfort had been concerned.

June 22, 1939

I was deep into the *Heckler and Wolf* when a
Marine knocked on my door and informed me
that a British soldier wished to speak with me.
The soldier entered the room, saluted smartly,
then asked to see my identification. I showed
him my ID, and he handed me a long cardboard
tube, then saluted and left. Inside the tube was a
large graph of the table of organization for the
German Army, with the names and dates of the
senior commanding officers written in pencil.

Mosby had the information copied by our
communications team and, at my request, sent
it to the office of the Chief of Staff. I wanted to
thank my benefactor, but Mosby advised me to
say nothing.

June 23, 1939

The day of the Army maneuvers. Felix called
for me at 0300, both of us in uniform, and I
carried a clip board. We drove to the railway
station, parked and purchased our train tickets.
It was a local train, so it took two hours to reach
Wuendsdorf, our destination, a lonely, deserted
station in the middle of nowhere. Our

transportation was waiting for us, an ancient Sd.Kfz 232 troop carrier (*Heckler and Wolf*), and we climbed in for a tooth-jarring half hour ride to a recently erected reviewing stand. We were to first officers to arrive, and, while Felix was off chatting with the German enlisted men, I slumped down on a folding wooden chair in the front row and promptly fell asleep.

An overhead noise awoke me. By this time, many of the other attachés had arrived and were seated behind me in the stand.

I heard someone call out "Fw 190." These were fighter planes overhead. Since the sky was cloudy, I couldn't see all of them but took the other attaché's word for their identity and marked down on my clip board the time they appeared and the estimated number. Shortly after, low flying dive bombers appeared. In my *Heckler & Wolf* they were called "Ju 87, (Stuka)" so I used this designation, together with the time and estimated number. As they dove, they emitted a terrible screeching noise, which carried to us, although the target was off in the distance.

Then the tanks rolled up. I was surprised to see that they were mostly light tanks (Pz II's and some Pz III's), mounting 20-40 mm guns. There were relatively few medium Pz IV's, some with 40mm, but most with 75mm, although light tanks predominated. Apparently, they were in the process of replacing the lights with the mediums, but the process was far from complete.

The tanks all trailed a wire, suggesting (to me) an antenna, and since they maneuvered in unison, it seemed likely that they had radio communication with the tank commander. Nothing I saw suggested a communication with the airplanes flying overhead. Also, I saw that a few of the Pz IV's had apparently broken down, and their drivers were waiting for a tow (?). Some of the tanks stopped, long enough for the driver to jump out with an oil can, but I could not see what they were doing with it. I assume they were oiling the bearings.

I overheard one of the Rumanian attachés speaking with Col. Jozsef Kodaly, the Hungarian, about the Pz II. The gist was that he thought the Polish 7tp was superior to the

German lights. I resolved to question him further—when I could do so discretely.

Off to the flanks were a few self-propelled cannon, which a voice behind me identified as the 88's. Actually, they have an easily identifiable silhouette. Some were drawn by a 18-ton half-track, but most were drawn by horse. Horse-drawn! How can they keep up with the Panzer advance? My answer: they can't, unless the panzer stops, long enough for the horse-drawn artillery to overtake them. So, for a while at least, the armored column will lack 88mm defense. Also, according to the *Heckler & Wolf*, these 88's were designed for anti-aircraft defense, but the barrels were pointed forward, not skyward. Major Zoran Pasic, the affable Yugoslavian, sitting behind me, commented to another attaché, that in the Spanish Civil War they were used as anti-tank guns, and they worked well.

One of the tankers left his tank and appeared to be waiting or something. An Opel truck loaded with 5-gallon metal containers quickly off-loaded 15 of those containers, whose contents the tanker began to pour into the gas tank. This intrigued me. This practice obviated the need for a special fuel tanker; fuel could be delivered more quickly in the 5-gallon cans. I resolved to make a special note of this.

I saw many half-track, open vehicles, with a 37mm gun projecting from the turret. These, the Swedish attaché explained to me, were some of the Sonderkraft vehicles and the one I pointed to was the Sd.Kfz. 251 Hanomag 251. What they are is an infantry transport vehicle, carrying 10 infantrymen, which keeps up with the Panzers and provides immediately available infantry support for urgent tasks, such as clearing minefields, capturing pillboxes, etc. The regular infantry units are far behind, so they cannot be relied on for immediate help. The American army, to my knowledge, has no similar vehicle, and I resolved to include mention of the Sonderkraft in my forthcoming reports.

Mobile support followed: command, medical, supply, repair. I could not identify all the units but composed as best a description as I could. Dust was beginning to choke the spectators. Cognac flasks appeared. An announcement was made that a refreshment table had been set up behind the reviewing stand, and all of the attachés, except myself filed out. I remained seated in my chair and continued to make notes, and where I could not recognize the item, I made a crude sketch, to help with later identification.

And now came the Infantry: in trucks, on motorcycles, on foot and even on bicycles (of all things), everyone trying to keep up with the armored column.

Finally, the horses: some with riders but most drawing wagons or cannon. On and on came the horses. Two, then three hours passed, and still the cavalcade of horses. By now, the cloud of dust had thickened, and many of the attachés had long departed.

Felix had spent most of the time joking with the German soldiers, and I heard them laughing at the back of the reviewing stand, where a flask of liquor was being passed around. The attachés had been forbidden to take photographs, so they had to put away their expensive cameras. Except for Felix. He had an ancient folding Kodak with patched (!) bellows, which he used to take pictures of the reviewing stand, the attachés and the soldiers. Towards late dusk, we were informed that the last transport to the train station was ready to leave, so I gathered my notes. The soldiers talking to Felix seemed a little tipsy.

June 28, 1939

I have been carefully studying German Army organization, particularly the Panzer division and hope I got it right. The organization of the Panzer division was not consistent, but, in general, goes something like this. The Panzer division consists of one Panzer brigade composed of two tank regiments; and a brigade of motorized infantry and a brigade of artillery. In other words, the Panzer division is fundamentally one tank brigade with non-tank components! Or at least that's how it appears to me at present. This may have to be revised!

July 8, 1939

Towards noon, as I was correcting my notes with a *H & W* booklet opened before me, a visitor appeared. He was Georg Dobring, the German Foreign Office liaison officer, selected, no doubt, because he was also a reserve Army lieutenant. Georg was a likable, dark haired fellow in his late twenties, dressed in a well-tailored business suit with a stiff, detachable shirt collar.

He explained that he had just returned from his tour of duty with his regiment, so could not have come sooner. It was his job to ensure that the new attaches were "settled in." Berlin has many recreational facilities, both at the embassies and in the city, and he would be happy to make arrangements for anything that strikes my fancy: bridge? poker? gambling? chess? football? swimming? etc. etc. On and on he went, and I said no to all of them. Exasperated, he recalled that he had read somewhere that the West Point cadet was expected to excel in at least one sport and asked me what mine was.

Caught! I had to tell him it was fencing.

Fencing! For heaven's sake! He was a fencer, he exclaimed, and belonged to the most prestigious fencing club in Germany. They had won two gold medals in the 1936 Olympics! He insisted that I come and see his fencing club.

There was no easy way out. I followed him to his old Mercedes and we drove to the Charlottenburg district and parked. The club was a large, pretentious building surrounded by pillars, something like a Prussian version of a small Parthenon. Inside was a hall with glass cabinets filled with cups, ribbons and medals; and on the walls hung pictures of old European fencing matches, with a brass plate affixed to it giving the details.

My eyes almost leaped out of their sockets when we came to the picture of the 1924 fencing Olympics, There was Mr. Genomi, my coach at West Point, foil fencing as a young man in the finals against his good friend and comrade (I forgot his name). Mr. Genomi came home with a silver, his friend took the gold.

Georg brought me into the dressing room and called to a man standing near a sink, dressed in a short white coat. The man approached us. He was in his late fifties, a wiry, thoughtful man with a receding hair line. He was introduced as a Mr. Kubris, and his name sounded familiar. Then it came to me. He was the man my fencing master at West Point told us about!

They had met in international fencing matches while Mr. Genomi was studying at Bologna. He told us that Kubris was the greatest fencer (foil) of his day.

I greeted him and started to tell him how often my coach had spoken of Edvard Kubis, when he shook his head and looked away. Something was wrong.

Georg had him fix me up, and Kubis selected the appropriate equipment from the visitor's closet. Usually, I'm reluctant to use another's gear, but these items looked scrupulously clean. I donned my fencing apparel, and Georg retrieved his from his locker. He had me sign the visitor's log, giving my name, title (always) and home address. George led me into the large fencing *saal*, bristling with the sounds of scraping and clashing steel. There were 5 long strips on which 10 or so matches were in progress, most foil and one saber. Most of the fencers were just sparring, but a few formal matches were in progress, with a judge officiating.

One of the foil matches attracted my attention. A tall, aggressive fencer was paired off against a slower, more cautious man. Around the strip were a dozen minions observing the match. With every point the big fellow scored, his claque cheered discretely. Both were competent, but neither excelled.

Georg and I found a place at the far end of a strip. I usually spend a hour warming up, but today I had no desire to hang around. My plan was to have him attack, while I would merely retreat, parry and riposte. In other words, let him knock himself out. He wasn't much of a fencer, but he was enthusiastic and kind-hearted and deserved some indulgence.

Fifteen minutes of uninspiring fencing slipped by, and one of the minions from the other match approached us to say that Commander Heydrich invites Captain Manning for a match. He was anxious to see what an American can do.

Georg almost had a heart attack. He whispered that I must go; that he's head man, after Himmler. I had heard of Himmler. He was the chief of the S.D. (secret service, Gestapo, etc.). His name was whispered.

I followed the messenger to the other patch.
The "head man" had removed his mask,
revealing a handsome, blond, man, perhaps in
his late thirties. His thin lips and set jaw seemed
to suggest arrogance. I knew I could beat him in
a heartbeat, but the question was, did I want to?
I had been told not to stir the pot, but this
fellow badly needed to be set straight.

Mr. Genomi had always taught that the most
important move for a fencer is "attack, lunge!"
In fact, he had us lunging for three months (!)
before he began teaching the upper limb
maneuvers. Three months!

What should I do? Imprudence won out. I
resolved to teach this big shot a quick lesson,
and see where it goes. We saluted each other.

"*En guard!*" said the judge.

I stepped back slightly, but then lunged forward
with as much lightening as I could muster—as
fast as when I was last in training 5 years ago.

"Halt!" cried the judge and tilted his head
toward me, indicating that I had won the point.
The minions looked ill at ease.

"En guard!"

I repeated the same attack with competition speed, but this time my foil tip bent when I touched him, and I held it there for all to see. They saw it all right, and I saw them squirming with an embarrassed look.

But there's such a thing as going too far, and I had gone as far as prudence would allow. We resumed fencing again, but now I returned to what I had been doing with Georg: retreat, parry-riposte, with no intention of scoring a point (however easy it could have been). I kept him moving and gave him a workout within his competency for 20 minutes, without letting him score.

A black-uniformed SS soldier appeared and spoke to the judge. The judge raised his hand to halt the match. The messenger then spoke to the fencer and left. Heydrich handed his foil and mask to an onlooker and informed us that he had to go.

He started to leave, then turned around and thanked me for the "lesson." Georg and I went back to our strip and fenced for another twenty minutes before calling it a day. In the locker room, Kubis had gone and another attendant had taken his place.

On the way back to the embassy, Georg brought me up to date. Edvard Kubis, he explained, had been the club's fencing master until he made a few incautious remarks about the Nazi invasion of Czechoslovakia. He was arrested; but the club officers persuaded Himmler himself to release him. Of course, Georg lost his job as fencing master, and Heydrich was waiting for another opportunity to pull him in. Georg, I gather, was no Nazi enthusiast.

Back at the embassy, Bradford and Mosby listened attentively to my story and assessed the consequences. At length Bradford turned to me and said that he thinks I did well. And added, "I hope."

July 9, 1939

Mosby has posted a newsletter on the bulletin board in the canteen. "The United States has occupied Iceland." Most of us assume it was done to shorten the sea lanes to Britain, previously requiring British naval protection.

July 10, 1939

While hard at work on the table of organization, Helen brought in an envelope from the Mexican embassy and laid it on my desk. In it was a brief note from Felix: "Thought you might like to have these." It contained beautiful photographs of some of the tanks and equipment we saw during the review. The son-of-a-gun had managed to take photos, where the other attachés had failed. Two of the photos showed the drivers inspecting the tank tracks of a stalled Pz IV, and one showed the delivery of the 5-gallon containers. I had the photos sent to Washington with an identification of where, when and by whom the photos had been taken.

Noontime, another letter arrived, brought in by a messenger in black, SS uniform. He handed me the envelope, followed by a stiff "Heil Hitler" salute.

My name was on the envelope in beautiful English calligraphy. Inside, was a handwritten invitation to an informal Sunday night soirée at the home of Mr. and Mrs. Commander ("Obengruppenfuhrer") Heydrich.

I had the messenger wait for an answer. Bradford and Mosby were in the vicinity. I showed them the invitation, and they discussed the matter before coming to a decision.

"O.K.," said Bradford. "You go!" He instructed me to accept the invitation on embassy stationary. I was to go in civilian clothes and avoid lengthy discussions. Vincent would drive me there, and I was to get out of the car 5 minutes before 8 pm. Not later, not earlier. I would see why. Also, Vincent would wait and drive me back. Bradford and Mosby would wait up for me. He concluded by begging me to stay out of trouble.

I wrote the response on embassy paper and handed it to the messenger, who favored me with another "Heil Hitler" and left. Not being in uniform, I was under no obligation to return the salute.

In preparation for the soiree, I had my dark suit ironed by Trudi. Sleep did not come easy.

July 11, 1939

By 7:15 pm the limousine was already waiting for me in the inner court of the embassy. Bradford had given me last minute instructions that did nothing to calm me down. The ride was to Charlottenburg, an affluent residential area. Vincent pointed to the house, an elegant mansion, surrounded by a high iron fence. There were many *grosse* Mercedes (big cars) parked in the vicinity. Vincent pulled in as close as he could to the home, and we waited.

At 7:55pm I got out of the car and saw people leaving the other vehicles at the same exact time. A line quickly formed leading to the door. When I crossed the threshold, I gave my name and title to a servant. The receiving line moved quickly. As I approached the Heydrichs, the servant announced: "Captain Brian Manning, US Army."

The wife welcomed me, but Heydrich was more demonstrative. He identified me as the Fencing champion of the United States and bade me a Good Evening, *Meister* (master). With that, I was passed to the next receiver.

The living room and the hall filled up rapidly, mostly with black-uniformed SS men, and a few older men in civilian dress. The serving table was crowded, so I stayed away. Several servants circulated with flutes of bubbling German (?) champagne, but no mineral water.

The crowd nudged me into the hallway, past a room with an open door. I caught a glimpse of book cases and a few music stands scattered about. In front of the bay window a man was seated in a high-backed easy chair, holding a large music folio. He wore a yellow sleeveless sweater over a tie-less white shirt, open at the collar. He called to me to sit down.

He knew my name from Reinhardt Heydrich, and also knew that I was 1934 American foil fencing champion. He told me l that his home was directly opposite the garden we faced. As best as I could tell, he had a thoughtful look, a pleasant smile and a cultured voice. No doubt he ate babies for breakfast.

His name was Canaris and remarked that I speak German like a native. Where was my father born? I told him Nauhut, Germany. He had never heard of it.

Since he was holding a music folio, I asked if he were a musician? Only an amateur musician, he told me; he tilled other fields for his livelihood. Was my family musically inclined? I replied that my grandmother was a famous pianist named Louise de Chevny and asked if he had heard of her. He had, indeed, and owned an early record of de Chevny, playing the Chopin *Etudes*. "Even with the scratching, it sounds magnificent."

We chatted a while. He entertained me with his ribald adventures in Chile during the war, when he and some English officers, also on parole, ran wild around Valparaiso. Had their respective navies heard about them, they surely would have been court-martialed on their return. We talked a while longer, until the noise in the hall reminded me that people were preparing to leave.

As he got up to go, he told me that I may hear from him, if he learns anything about my family. And with that he opened the bay window and began walking across the garden.

The departure line moved swiftly: A "Thank you for your kind invitation;" a handshake; a photo flash, and I was out the door. Vincent had orders to take me back to the embassy, where I reported to my waiting audience.

Canaris, Mosby told me, is Admiral Wilhelm Canaris, chief of the Abwehr (intelligence). According to Kirstin Bradford, he has the reputation of being a decent man—as opposed to his friend, Heydrich, who is better known as "the hangman." All in all, they told me, I did well.

Vincent took me back to my lodging, and I had no difficulty falling asleep.

July 13, 1939

A handwritten letter came today from Admiral Wilhelm Canaris, written on Abwehr stationary (which Mosby kept):

> *"Dear Captain,*
>
> *The town, Nauhut, where your family comes from, was given to Poland and is now called Nowa Divor. Its former German population has long since departed.*

*A Kurt von Manig left on the SS Rostock
from Cuxhaven, Germany on July 6, 1906
bound for Boston, Massachusetts. On arrival to
the United States, he became Charles Manning.*

*I take pleasure in informing you that
you have a first cousin living in Berlin, Colonel
Paul von Manig, a personal friend. Allow me
the pleasure of notifying him of your presence.*

With warm regards,

Canaris"

I showed the letter to Bradford and asked him
what I should do.

"Wait," I was told.

July 20, 1939

A hand-delivered letter was sent up to me by
the marine sentry.

"Dear Captain Manning,

*My husband, Colonel Paul von Manig, and I
are very anxious to meet you before my
husband's leave expires.*

Would it be convenient for you to come to our home at 140 Victoria Louise Street on this Monday at 8:30 pm or on any other night at your convenience, but hopefully it will be soon.

With respect,

Caterine von Manig (Mrs. Colonel)

I showed the letter to my bosses, who showed it to Kirstin, who had just come into the room. They had no objection to my going. Mosby knows the von Manig family. They send their son to the same school as Clayton. Further instructions: business suit, flowers for the wife—a small bouquet—nothing too fancy.

July 22, 1939

I set out early by underground and streetcar to the Wilmersdorf section. From an old woman selling flowers at a street stand, I bought a small bouquet, but, truthfully, the bunch looked a little ragged, and I regretted not having visited the florist shop near the embassy. The address brought me through a middle-class district to a somewhat decrepit residential building which had lost its former elegance.

A sign was posted in front: "This building has been condemned and is subject to demolition." The date given was long past. The right side of the building was sagging badly, and a small area of the wall had collapsed. The vestibule had no doorman and a yellow tape was strung along the right side of the lobby, shutting off access to the elevator. From the name directory posted on the wall, I learned that the von Manigs were living on the first (European second) floor. At precisely 8:30 pm I knocked on the door.

A flurry of footsteps from within, and the door was opened by a thin, dark-haired man in his forties, behind whom stood two nervous women and a boy. Both woman wore brightly crocheted aprons, which I immediately recognized.

I was invited in and introduced by Paul von Manig to his wife, Caterine; his sister-in-law, Dr. Elisabet de Talligny; and his son Frederick. "And don't call me Fritz!" added the eleven-year-old in perfect English.

On the wall beside the small entrance vestibule was a picture of Hitler, like in most German households, but the electric light had not been turned on. They led me into the parlor, where I dutifully presented my bouquet to the Frau Colonel. I could see that the furnishings were well-worn and long past their prime. I sat on a worn sofa, and the boy sat next to me. The adults pulled up easy chairs in front of the couch.

The wife asked if I would like something to drink and suggested tea, since they do not drink alcohol. I could feel my heart thumping. Nor did my parents drink alcohol, I told her. My mother wore an apron just like hers. She came from Lorain and belonged to the French Protestant (Huguenot) Church.

Caterine replied that she and 'Sabette were both born in Lorraine. Sabette still attends the French Protestant Church here in Berlin, but she and her husband are Lutheran congregants, as are most of the officers in his regiment. I told them my mother's name, Paula De Chevny, the daughter of the pianist. Caterine knew the family; the de Chevnys came from the Moselle region. The preliminaries over, she asked her husband to show me the photo album.

The old photo album was produced, with pictures held in place by embossed paper hinges. By now, the photographs were badly faded. Paul came up behind the sofa and explained each photo. He pointed to the three brothers as children: Kurt, the eldest, (my father); next Wilhelm and lastly Max, (Paul's father). We had long since unconsciously abandoned the formal "you" ("Sie") and had drifted to the familiar "Du."

My father, Kurt, was sent at great expense to the famous Friedrich Wilhelm High School in Berlin. Somewhere toward the end of his studies, he decided he did not want the life of a Prussian land owner, so he ran away to the States. The next oldest, Wilhelm, died in the war; the youngest, Max, Paul's father, survived the war, married and begot Paul. After the war, their property was lost when, by the terms of the Versailles Treaty, parts of East Prussia were turned over to Poland.

He pointed to each photograph, one by one, and explained each. I saw photos of my grandfather, my grandmother, my father as a boy atop a horse, my father as a schoolboy, the other sons.

The photos were faded, but they conveyed hallowed meaning. These were my family, my people!

They asked about my parents. I described their lives and my father's success. I did not mention that he died one of the richest men in America and that his wealth has since doubled. As for myself, I had little of interest to tell them: undistinguished Army officer, unmarried, unsettled, unexceptional.

Caterine's sister, Elisabet, in a word, was the prettiest woman I had ever met or hope to meet. She wore a dark, well-tailored suit and white shirt, partially concealed by her apron. Her hair was set in a rather old-fashioned bun and she wore only trace of lipstick to complement her clear blue eyes. When she spoke, her voice radiated warmth and gentleness. In short, for me it was, love at first sight. What a night!

Meanwhile, the boy had fallen asleep. Paul carried him upstairs to his bedroom, and I reminded myself that Elisabet had to work tomorrow. She is some kind of foreign service officer with consular rank that takes her to places around the world; but her present assignment is here in Berlin at the Ministry of Foreign Affairs. Somewhat reluctantly, I prepared to leave. They begged me to return often, especially since Paul will soon be departing. She explained that when her son was off at school, Caterine spends most of her time searching for a new home, since the present building is scheduled to be demolished. Contrary to popular belief, the German Colonel's salary is not great, unless he happens to be a party member (like Erwin Rommel), in which case the rewards could be boundless.

Since the hour was late, I returned directly to my lodging, rather than the embassy. It was an earthshaking experience for me—meeting my family and, God willing, my future wife, if I dare say it.

August 1, 1939

This morning, for the first time, I saw the yellow arm band, which is now compulsory for the Jews. The police pass along the row of people lined up outside the consular office, insuring that all are properly identified. One of the regular policemen, an old fellow, saw me staring at the line. He looked at me sadly and shook his head.

August 15, 1939

The noise in the streets has become intolerable, especially outside the propaganda ministry down the sreeet. Not only do the loud speakers blare out their hateful accusations against Poland, but the streets are filled with marching soldiers and bands, all moving eastward. We learn from the BBC in the Mosby apartment that the British government has served notice that Britain will go to war if Germany invades Poland. This, the *Berliner Zeitung* and the *Frankfurter Algemeine Zeitung* both ridicule.

Paul has left Berlin and has returned to his division. I try to visit every night, but not before Fred has finished his homework. I bring them chocolate, tea, coffee and pastries, items imported from Denmark by the embassy and not available to the Berlin household.

Fred ("Fritz") knows the Mosby boy. In fact they are in the same classes. Both are gifted students; or at least, smarter than I was at their age.

Still no luck with Caterine finding a house or apartment. If anything, homes are harder to find, since Hitler's architect has been tearing down buildings to make way for Germania, the future glorious capital of the Third Reich. Caterine has had several apartments shown her that had belonged to Jewish families, but has refused them all. I did not pursue the subject. Being an American military attaché, I must not let such things concern me.

August 20, 1939

The visa applicants are backed up into Pariser Platz and I am called upon to interview. What a terrible feeling knowing that the U.S. quotas have already been filled and that nothing can be done for these people. Still, I must do something to earn my keep, since my present activities as a military attaché have not yet been especially productive.

This evening I went to another attaché meeting. Gradually, my knowledge of military matters has been expanding. The outspoken Major Zoran Pasic, the Yugoslavian, made an interesting point. When someone remarked that he did not believe that Hitler will attack Poland,

Zoran replied that he will attack because he needs gold. He's taken it from Austria, Czechoslovakia, and the Jews, but now his gold supply has run out. He needs more. Poland is next! Rather simplistic, but we will see, won't we?

August 21, 1939

Early visit to my family. Elisabet and Fred have not yet returned, and Caterine was dressed for a social call. It seems that the other apartment owner in the building, Mr. and Mrs. Goldberg, want to prepare tea for us. Caterine had given them some of the tea I had brought for her, and they wanted to show their appreciation. I dislike being put in this situation, but said nothing and followed Caterine.

On the way down to the apartment, Caterine told me about the family. They used to make slippers and had done so for a hundred years. They have a letter from Bimarck's secretary thanking them for the comfortable pair Bismarck wears around his estate at Varsin. Now, the Goldbergs have been notified that they will be expelled from Berlin to a resettlement center.

This is the kind of situation I have been warned about and told to avoid. But I couldn't leave now.

The Goldbergs received us, a retiring bourgeois couple, living with bourgeois furniture, and with bourgeois paintings on the walls. I saw a packed valise near the door, which is said to be present in every Jewish household awaiting expulsion orders. While the wife was pouring the tea, the man told us that he had long ago submitted a visa application to our embassy and hoped to hear from them soon. Poor fellow, if he only knew how hopeless their situation was.

There was a heavy pounding on the door, and Mrs. Goldberg opened it. In walked an aggressive, surly man, who announced that he was sent by the Gauleiter's office. His name was Eugen Slichter and his job was to appraise the furniture and contents, which he proceeded to do. Max and Sibel Goldbergs, he said, are scheduled for relocation in two weeks' time. He walked around the rooms, opening and inspecting drawers and making notes on his pad. When he finished, he announced that the furniture was now officially the property of the

Gauleiter, Joseph Goebbels. Nothing could be sold or given away.

We tried to resume the tea drinking. Out of the blue, Mr. Goldberg asked about the weather in Rochester, New York

Rochester? Why Rochester? Why not Detroit or San Francisco? It turns out that Goldberg's son lives in Rochester and together, they own a slipper factory in that city.

My stomach turned. I used an excuse to leave and rushed back to the embassy. I went directly to the consular section. The day was winding down and most of the staff had left, but I found the consul, Tim Murphy, still hanging around and followed him into his office.

I asked him to get out the application of Max and Sibel Goldberg, dated April 21, 1937, resident of Berlin.

Required Documentation: applications, fees, police waivers, sponsors, custodial bonds, open-date steamship tickets. After 10 minutes, he returned with a taped folder, on the cover of which someone had written "complete.". He sat down, opened the folder, sorted out the pages, consulted the checklist and confirmed that the application was indeed "complete."

Tim was puzzled. From his view, it was all here. What about it?

I told him that Mr. Goldberg is part owner of a factory in Rochester, New York, and Tim nearly went through the roof. He shuffled through the papers, came to the last page, read it and gasped, stood up and then sat down.

The interviewer had missed the last page.

Special consideration is given to applicants who own property in the U.S.

I told him to get the visa to the Goldbergs by this evening, but he shook his head. We reached an agreement. He would put the visa in their hands tomorrow, and I would say nothing of this to the Consul General.

August 22, 1939

In Mittelkamp Book Store the maps of Poland and the Polish travel books are all sold out, if that means anything. At Mosby's suggestion, I mentioned this in a short note to the Deputy Chief of War Plans, Office of the Chief of Staff.

I visit my family every night. Sometimes we play bingo, much to the delight of Fred, whose joyful shriek warms my heart. Elisabet still refuses to go with me to the opera, the theater, or anywhere in public. Caterine says it would fatally jeopardize her position at the Foreign Ministry.

August 26, 1939

Some things about Mosby I cannot understand. His sole duties are confined to the embassy, which seems rather restrictive for a senior Marine Corps captain. Also, he wears a West Point class ring (!). Shouldn't it be an Annapolis ring, if he's a Marine Corps captain? If we were in the States, I could look him up in an instant in the nearest reference room, but here in Berlin there is no such thing (except perhaps in Canaris' Abwehr library).

Also, I saw a photograph of Franklin Roosevelt hanging in an out-of-the way corner of his living room. The light was bad, but I think it was inscribed, "To my loyal friend and neighbor with great thanks." What do you make of that?

Lastly, he keeps closed, under lock and key, the door to a room in his apartment, in which none of us mortals are allowed to enter, not even his wife or son. On one occasion, I heard a peculiar noise coming from it that sounded like a printing press. If someone has a reasonable explanation, explain it to me.

August 23,1939

A bombshell has exploded in the German press. Hitler and Stalin have signed a non-aggression pact! My colleagues seem to think that Hitler will now be free to invade Poland.

According to the *Berliner Zeitung*, Britain & France will do nothing, just as they did nothing when the German Army moved into Czechoslovakia. Paris Square, just outside our embassy, is filled with troops and vehicles moving east. With harrowing repetition, the loud speakers blast out reports of Polish atrocities against the German women in Danzig, whipping the population into a frenzy.

August 28, 1939

Further forebodings. I received a telephone call from Colonel Scott-Comfort, the British attaché, inviting me to his home this evening. He lives on Bluecher Street in the northwest part of the city (Wellcome District), not too far from my lodgings, but requiring two street car rides to get there, (or an S train and a tram).

The house was in an upper-middle class residential area, but, even with its three stories, it was smaller than the other houses on the street. Two annexes projected from the home, both appearing to have been built at the same time as the home itself. The windows were completely blacked out, in conformity to the air raid regulations; and the shutters drawn. The lawns were small, but seemed adequately maintained.

I knocked on the door and was admitted by a middle-aged man servant, who held out a card tray. As I fumbled for my card wallet, the voice of the colonel rang out: "Come in, Captain. Welcome." He was informally dressed in a smoking jacket. I was led into a library-office in one of the annexes, and he shut the door. The annex was divided into a study, where we were seated, and beyond it, a bed room. Perhaps one of the early occupants had the annex built to avoid having to climb the stairs to the upper floor.

After I had settled down and refused a cognac, he told me he had two important matters to discuss. First, Germany will invade Poland on September 1st and Britain will shortly thereafter declare war. I started to reply, but he interrupted and assured me that it was a fact; and, since the British embassy people will be interned while they await repatriation, he will have to leave before hostilities begin.

The reason he has sent for me, he went on, is this. To date, their source of their secret information has been absolutely trustworthy. Perhaps the informant is an employee of the German Foreign Office; he doesn't know. What is important is that the source has told him that he is willing to work with the U.S. embassy people.

This is how it works. Do I know that cafe on Wessel Street, not far from our embassy? I nodded. It was called Danau Konditorei. He continued: there's a small toy lion laying on its side in the show window. If the lion is laying on its side—no messages. When the lion stands upright, I enter the place around 11 am, take a newspaper from the rack and go to the right side of the cafe to a two-place table and sit down. The place will not be busy then, so I will have my choice of tables. I order and pay for a beer. Make sure there is an ash tray on the table.

Around noon time, people will begin pouring in from the nearby offices, and the place will fill. Incidentally, the Foreign Office is not far away. A little man, with a wing collar and a folded newspaper will approach me and ask if he can be seated. I nod. He will sit down, pull out a cigar, remove the cigar band, roll it up in his fingers and put it in the ash tray.

A few minutes later, I casually reach for the band; put it in my coat pocket and leave. The message will be hand-written in English in very small letters. How he does that, I do not know. It will require a hand lens to read it.

Something out of a Somerset Maugham story. He repeated the procedure again to ensure I had understood it, and for good measure raced though it a third time, as if I were a school boy.

At this point, he offered a cup of tea, and I declined.

Next, he went on to say that he is forced to sell his home. Perhaps I know of someone in my embassy—"

I asked for a description of the house. The main floor had two annexes: the one we were in now with the bedroom and study; and the other with kitchen and living quarters for the two servants, Therese ("Resi") and Bruno Geulen. The house had three floors, with the bedrooms on the second (American) floor, some of which had *en suite* bathrooms. On the floor above were the servant's rooms, which were at present unoccupied and unheated. Lastly, there were two coal-burning furnaces, one of which is being used.

The price? Quite reasonable for a home of this size in this part of the city and fully consistent with the values I had seen on the embassy bulletin board, when I searched, with the von Manigs in mind. I suppose I should have first consulted Director Weisbard, but this was an emergency situation requiring prompt judgment (something a good Army officer should have).

About the transfer of title formalities, nothing easier. He explained that the home was a "diplomatic house," and special arrangements had been made for embassy people. The property must be bought and sold with foreign money by non-German embassy people and is exempt from most of the taxes and regulations.

He produced several pages, partially filled out. The sole condition for the sale was that Resi and Bruno Geulen must remain with the house. I'll find them absolutely reliable in more ways than I can imagine.

By some incredible stroke of luck, this house was exactly what I needed and wanted. I wrote a check from the First National of Boston and drew out of my wallet the home telephone number of Director Weisbart who could verify-

He assured me that verification would not be necessary, since he knew all about me. After all, his ten years with British intelligence had been of some value.

After signing some papers, we concluded with a handshake, and he then introduced me to the couple. Resi Geulen was the archetypical Prussian servant, quiet, reserved (and observant), and her husband, Bruno, a few years older, ramrod straight, seemingly unimaginative and silent.

I described the other people who will be moving in. Mrs. Von Manig and her sister, Dr. de Talligny, come from Loraine, and have customs which may appear somewhat curious. You'll have to work it out. Also, I want Mrs. Guelen to hire a part-time cleaning woman, since she can't do everything herself. To Bruno Geulen, I said that he will need someone to tend the furnaces and the landscaping. He knew just the right man, his old war comrade. The house has a small room in the basement where the furnace man can sleep.

Scott-Comfort spent another half hour giving me advice and, after handing me the deeds and key, went back to finish the packing. I think it unlikely we will ever meet again,

August 24, 1939

My *demenagement* from the von Huzic lodgings went smoothly. The chamber maids helped me pack, I said my goodbyes and my gear was carried by horse and wagon to my new home. Resi helped me unpack. Fortunately, my bedroom had a closet for the clothing, so I was spared a wardrobe.

Late afternoon I arrived at the von Manig residence. Caterine and Fred were in the parlor, and Elisabet had just come home. They knew immediately that something important had happened. I told them about the house and the living arrangements. This is something my father would have wanted, I explained that I must nominally remain the owner, but that Caterine will be the chatelaine and run the house. At some happier time in the future, I promise to transfer the title to Paul. As a practical matter, an account was being set up at the German Commercial bank so that Caterine and Elisabet could run the house and pay for repairs. Also, I left the stack of papers and asked Elisabet to run through them to ensure that all the necessary actions have been taken.

If additional help is required, Dr. Weisbart would be happy to assist.

I hinted—although reluctant to do so—that my father had left me rather well off.

Since the new home is adequately furnished, there was little need to bring their furniture. Most of their furnishings can readily be sold, since new furniture was no longer being manufactured. I wrote down the new address and telephone number and left, without waiting for their reaction.

At the attaché meeting, there was a large Michelin map of Poland spread out on a table, and around it the attachés gathered to point and comment.

The Rumanian attaché, Colonel Claudiu Popa, told me something about the Polish tank. I should add that Romania is an ally of Poland, and Col. Popa has served as an observer with a Polish armored company. Contrary to what I had believed, the Polish 7tp is a very serviceable tank. It has strong armor made from hardened steel alloy, reinforced with chromium and nickel. Its diesel engine is something of a drawback since its fuel supply is not always available. It achieves a higher velocity with its 37 mm gun than does the German Pz II. Unfortunately, the Poles have too few tanks and what they do have are seldom massed in battalion strength, but are scattered around the infantry. Lastly, the 7tp lacks radio communication, so that a concentrated attack is difficult (if not impossible)..

August 31, 1939

No more *Herald Tribune*, but the BBC still broadcasts, and Mosby has arranged for the communications department to publish a one-page newsletter of current events based on the news broadcasts from New York, for our embassy people and whoever else wants a copy.

The military attachés meet every night. They plot on a large table map the last known location of German army units mentioned in the recent communiqués and we speculate on their next move.

Also, they talk about American politics (though discouraged from doing so). FDR is being challenged for the third presidential term by someone named "Wendell Willkie," I saw a picture of him in a recent Time magazine. He looks to me like a dynamic leader, but most of the embassy think it unlikely that he can dislodge "the old bastard."

September 1, 1939

Germany has invaded Poland! War with France and Britain to follow. Throngs of people stream out of the Goebbels Propaganda ministry nearby. If one stares at their building long enough, you can see Goebbels himself arriving or departing in a huge limousine, surrounded by a crowd of posturing lackeys. Although quite small, he is clearly visible in the automobile as the rear seat had been elevated

The von Manig family has moved in after only a few wagon trips. I tried to come home after everyone had retired, to give Caterine a chance to run the show unhindered. Only Bruno stayed up to greet me. I told him that henceforth he need not do so, unless I specifically asked him to.

September 2, 1939

This morning, as I walked by the Danau cafe on my way to the embassy, I saw the lion standing upright. My bosses were duly notified. At 1100 I entered the *konditorei*, selected a newspaper, sat at an appropriate table and ordered (ersatz) coffee. I waited and waited. An hour later, as the place began to fill up, a small man wearing a wing collar approached my table and asked if he could sit down. I nodded. He sat, ordered, took off the cigar band from his cigar, rolled it up and put it in the ash tray. I retrieved it and left.

At the embassy, Mosby unrolled the band, and we examined it with a hand lens. "The Soviet Union will enter Poland on September 17, 1939." Fifteen days away—Washington will have plenty of advanced notice.

Mosby got up without comment and went to the communications room.

September 3, 1939

Breakfast with Fred before he went off to school. We sat in the kitchen, American style.

No need to eat in the dining room, even though places had been set there. I wonder how Caterine is getting on with the Geulens? First rate, I would guess, since Resi Geulen seems quite adaptable

According to the Nazi communiqués, the Germans armored columns have made tremendous gains. Moreover, the weather has been dry, which has been a great help to the Pz II, when fording a stream, since it cannot negotiate more than 1 meter of water. I thank my lucky stars that I had gone to the Panzer brigade exercise, for it gave me some accurate concepts about tank logistics.

September 17, 1939

The Russian Army has occupied the eastern half of Poland up to the town of Brest-Litovsk. The Germans seem to have four columns: Silesia and Slovakia in the south; and Pomerania and East Prussia to the north. The western armies (Silesia and Pomerania) seem to be converging, as are the eastern armies; but it is still too soon to be certain.

September 19, 1931

The first newsreels have been shown at a
nearby theater (which also featured a
Hollywood musical with Fred and Adele
Astaire). We see a German Panzer division on
the move carrying laughing infantrymen atop
the Pz IV tanks. No hint of concern.

At the Golden Hind, Zoran Pasic told us that he
has been "informed" (source undisclosed) that
the Pz III has been plagued by leaking oil; that
the Pz II has trouble extricating itself out of the
mud; and, also, that the German Army has a
shortage of track pins, so that if a pin
disappears, the tank commander has to wait for
the repair vehicle to bring a replacement. All
these may or not be true, in whole or in part,
but I listen. And report.

September 20, 1939

The Berlin newspapers are calling this a
"lightning war" (*Blitzkrieg*), and the BBC
seems to have picked up the term.

No word from Paul. He is still with his unit.
Where he is or what he does, he does not say.

September 22, 1939

At home, things seem to have settled down.
There are two name registers at the entrance,
Manning on one side and von Manig & de
Talligny on the other.

I have ordered a monopoly set from Sears for
Fred. Jean Mosby assures me that Fritz (I mean
Fred) can play the game. She knows the von
Manigs from Mrs. Robinson's school and likes
them very much.

The evening we had our first formal meal at our
new home. Dinner was early, so that Fred could
return to his school work. I have been bringing
home Danish stores and American cigarettes,
which Resi Geulen uses for trade. Caterine tells
me that Resi is a very canny haggler, so the
meal was quite good.

After dinner, we turned on our Telefunken
Radio and 'Sabette and I danced into the night.
Holding her in my arms was bliss. She uses no
perfume, no maquillage. I whispered in her ear
how much I adored her. Since I had never loved
like this before, I hope my words were
adequate.

Bruno Geulen has hired his war comrade, Albrecht, to tend our furnace and lawns, He had been badly shot up in the war and ever since, has not been right. He remains out of sight in the cellar and eats with the Geulens.

September 23, 1939

No word from Paul.

Caterine and Resi Geulen have apparently reached a detente. Resi brings the dishes to the serving stand; Caterine sets them on the dinner table. Both Caterine and Elisabet still wear their aprons and will not surrender their housfrau status.

Just as some attachés have predicted, two western columns (Army von Bock from Pomerania and Army von Rundstedt from upper Silesia) are converging west of Warsaw and will encircle the city. The newsreels show heavy artillery flattening Warsaw. Overhead, twin engine bomber planes release their bombs, destroying vast districts of the city. The pictures send a chill up my spine. I hope the German audiences will remember these scenes, if, and when destruction should ever come to their cities.

September 28, 1939

Warsaw has fallen! Unbelievable damage to the city. Great rejoicing in the streets of Berlin. "Hitler is a genius!" proclaims our visiting German barber at the embassy. The newsreels show the army in action, but it seems to me that most of the battle scenes are rehearsed.

Caterine has received a letter from Paul. Where he is and what he is doing are, of course, not mentioned. He has been promoted to General Major, which is equivalent to our Brigadier General. Resi has already made the change on the name register.

At the attachés' meeting, there was heavy discussion about the losses suffered by the German armor. The estimate is that 30% of the medium tanks were disabled, mostly from non-combat causes. Most of us accept that figure. Information from non-German sources is beginning to arrive. This information can be inconsistent. Some of it is fanciful; most, quite authentic. My job is to decide which is which.

October 1, 1939

Duncan Braford has been given two tickets to *Tristan und Isolde*, conducted by Karajan at the Stats Opera. Since Duncan dislikes Wagner, he offered the tickets to Dwaine, who also refused them; so, they were given to me; and I invited Helen. As a reward for attending, I was promised limousine service, courtesy of the U.S. Embassy.

I picked Helen up at her apartment house nearby. Both of us were formally dressed. Vincent brought us to the opera house and arranged to call for us after the performance.

Despite the audience's rapture, I had to keep myself from dozing off, and in fact did fall asleep in the third act. After the performance, we got our coats from the garderobe and went outside to wait for the embassy Cadillac.

There were no vehicles moving on the street. Someone said that the intersection was closed to street traffic for one hour.

One hour! Rather than hang around on the windy steps, we walked to a nearby tram booth, where we would at least have shelter from the wind. In the distance, we could see the sport stadium, all lit up. Why at this hour? We sat on the bench and waited for traffic to resume.

Suddenly, a line of trucks appeared on the intersecting boulevard. Instead of cargo, they carried loads of people, some of whom were women and crying children. The trucks seemed to be heading for a train station, a quarter of a mile away. Helen whispered that they were Jews. That explained the late hour.

We heard a noise from inside the waiting booth. A man had been sitting there in the dark, watching the procession. As he stood up and mounted his bicycle, we caught a glimpse of him. He wore overalls and a woolen hat and was carrying a stepladder on his shoulder. He looked familiar, very familiar. Had he stayed a minute longer, I would have called to him.

An hour later, Vincent appeared and delivered us to our respective residences.

Who was that bicycle rider? I kept turning the scene over and over in my mind. Then, as I was falling asleep, it came to me. Mosby! It could only have been Mosby! I think…Maybe.

October 8, 1939

Life at Bluecher Streer has been pure joy. We have dinner early, so Fred can get back to his homework. Later, we play family games, and we talk. Elisabet and I have formed a deep bond between us. I am so deeply in love that life without her is unthinkable. "I love you," I whisper to her as we sit in the living room after everyone has gone to sleep. Not only have I found my family in Berlin, but also my love.

October 9, 1939

I approached Bradford about the matter of marriage. Kirstin was also in the room, and answered for him. What I ask is impossible, she told me. The State Department will not consent to it, nor will the U.S. Army. Moreover, it will absolutely ruin the career of Dr. de Talligny. Perhaps worse than that. She is a Foreign Service officer, and the Nazis will never let her go. Never!

Mosby said the same. He begged me not to pursue this further, for the sake of my family.

I bide my time and wait.

October 10, 1939

From the many sources gathered by the attachés come reports of great cruelty done to the Polish population, some of which I find hard to believe. The senior attachés keep reminding us that we should discuss only military matters at the meetings. I, for one, find it hard to believe that the average German soldier would participate in the kind of cruelty that is described.

October 15, 1939

Paul has come home! The family is ecstatic. He can remain only a few days and then must return to his division. Mrs. Geulen has, by deft trading and *legerdemain,* acquired the ingredients to make a chocolate cake. This is despite the new regulations that require all ration book holders to register with only one grocer, who alone may deal with them.

Paul has been given a new Panzer brigade now being formed. I don't think he has had any previous Panzer experience, but he is a first-class officer and learns quickly. I would love to question him about his experiences, but that would be an unforgivable breech of military etiquette, and he would be forced to move out of our home.

I know nothing of Mosby's activities. I wish he would tell me what he does at night. Is it that he doesn't trust me? Or that I am too immature to understand? Whatever his activities, they seem to have the full support and endorsement of Bradford, who himself is something of a puzzle, as is Kirstin, his wife.

October 17, 1939

Paul has left today to rejoin his unit. The streets are still filed with military vehicles, but this time they are moving west. There are all kinds of speculation among the attaches. Few still think that Hitler will attack France immediately. The newspapers report vigorous building activity east of the Rhine along a new front facing the Maginot line. We see it in all the newsreels. The newspapers call it the Siegfried Line.

"'Hitler will attack!' says Zoran." I quote him, since he is the most outspoken of the attachés. The question is when. The German Army is not prepared for a winter campaign. Further, German losses in equipment during the Polish campaign—particularly in light tanks—must be replaced. According to the *Frankfort Algemeine Zeitung*, the Panzer factories will not run a three-shift production line; nor have women been called up for industry. Hitler seems mighty sure of himself with what he's got.

November 1, 1939

So far, there has been no military action in the west. The British newspapers call this inactivity a "sitzkrieg," instead of "blitzkrieg." The cabaret comedians laugh at the British. "Don't worry, Mr. Churchill," they crow, "you'll hear from us soon!"

The RAF flies over the German lines and drops propaganda leaflets instead of bombs. Meanwhile, winter approaches, and both sides try to keep warm.

November 2, 1939

Elisabet is being flown to Portugal to replace the German consul in Porto, who is scheduled to undergo surgery back home. I feel like going with her, never mind the consequences. What could a court-martial do to me, besides throw me in jail? If only that. Stupid idea.

November 15, 1939

For Thanksgiving, I invited the Mosbys, the Bradfords and the Cardenas to a Thanksgiving Dinner in my new home. Bradford declined, but the Cardenas accepted. Mosby accepted, but only on condition that he could be the chef. Places would be set for 9 in my household and 7 of the invitees, a total of 18 or so, which makes it a banquet. I gave Mosby the money for the meal and hoped for the best. With Mosby, anything is possible.

Resi was shocked when I told her, but calmed down when she learned that Capt. Mosby would be responsible for the preparations. Capt. Mosby, I told her, would telephone his instructions. This should be good! He has had sufficient time to order from Denmark and of course, has all the facilities and utensils of the commissary kitchen in the embassy.

November 27, 1939

The day of our Thanksgiving dinner!

Paul came home late yesterday with his batman, Herman. The guests all arrived early. Clayton Mosby and Fritz were both dressed in Pilgrim costume from school. We stood around and drank delicious, home-made, Danish apple cider. Finally, dinner was announced and we all sat down at a large table, joined to which were two smaller tables all covered by white tablecloths. Picture this: Paul at the head, next to him Caterine and Fritz, then the Mosbys, the Cardenas, the Geulens, the baby nurse, Herman the batman, Albrecht, our ash man; and finally, Elisabet, with myself at the end.

Paul said grace in German, Felix in Spanish, Caterine in French, and myself in English. After God was duly thanked, Resi and Caterine rushed into the kitchen, and the first course was served.

Clayton began by reciting the Pilgrim's history in English. When it came to the rescue by Squantum, Fred jumped up and continued the story in German; and they raced each other to the end. Then the meal began.

At my end of the table, I talked with the Herman, the batman, a young farm boy, who was new to Army life. Albrecht, our furnace man turned out to have had a very fascinating life. For one thing, he was born in Luxembourg and spoke Lotharingian, a dialect also used by some country people in Lorraine. After the war, (in which he served in Bruno's regiment) he spent most of his life in Berlin, living on the streets, until Bruno helped him with his present job.

Bruno Geulen, too, had an interesting story. He had already attended a Thanksgiving dinner in 1918, when the officer he had worked for ended up on an armistice commission after the war. On Thanksgiving Day, the officer and his batman, Bruno, were both invited (absolutely unheard of), to a Thanksgiving dinner by the Americans, so he had had his first taste of Thanksgiving.

The talk and laughter went on for hours, when suddenly a knock on the door sounded and a puffed-up block inspector announced himself. I led him into the study and closed the door.

He began by saying that he knew this was a foreign house but added that there were German people living here and that, accordingly, he must—

Here, his hand struck a framed photo standing on a book shelve and knocked it off the ledge. He picked it up, looked at it and his eyes seemed to pop out of his head.

"Excuse me," he said, replacing the picture and backed out of the room. "Excuse me," he repeated, as he passed by the dinner table. Resi Geulen met him at the door and handed him a bag, which he gratefully accepted and left. I picked up the photo and examined it. It was the picture taken of Heydrich and myself at the receiving line of his home. Never an ill wind that blows no good. Everyone laughed when I explained what had happened. Paul sat grim-faced and said nothing.

The meal was a memorable success. Cleaning up went quickly, and Dwaine had arranged for an embassy truck to return the dishes and cooking utensils to the commissary.

December 3, 1939

BBC has announced that the Soviet Union has invaded the Karelia peninsular in Finland! It appears to be an attempt by the Soviets to obtain Finnish land to fortify the northern approach to Leningrad. The Soviet Union has the largest army in Europe, larger than all the other armies in Europe put together; and more tanks, although most of them are said to be obsolete, according to *Time* magazine, which is why the Russians wanted the Christie tank. The attachés give the Finns at best a week.

Captain Carlsson says that the Finns will resist to the end. The Karelia Peninsular is narrow and the Finns tough. At the American embassy, everyone is cheering for the Finns. After all, aren't they the only nation to repay their war debt? (Actually, the debt was contracted after the war, and it was for only six million dollars.)

December 20, 1939

The Finns are still holding out. "Told you," said Arvid Carlsson, proudly. Carlsson knows some Swedish fellow officers who are serving with the Finns as observers. I hope to get reliable information from him. he newsreels showed Finnish soldiers on skis, wrapped in white outer clothing to camouflage them in the snow. Most bets are against the Finns lasting for more than one month. Carlsson took some of the bets and begged me to cover the rest. I declined, remembering the caution to avoid controversy.

December 21, 1939

I heard Major Claudiu Popa, the Rumanian, mentioning to another attaché that the Soviet troops he saw in the newsreels wore reservist uniforms and were not regular Soviet army. I don't know what that means, if indeed it is true, but Rumania has nothing to gain by inventing this report. Might it mean that the Soviets are using the Finnish campaign as an exercise to train their men, or is the report a hoax? I mentioned the matter to Mosby, and he advised me to send a brief note to Washington and let them decide.

December 23, 1939

For the first time, we see clusters of emaciated, badly clothed Poles working in the streets. Always with SS oversight. They are housed in the most miserable buildings or in crude canvas coverings resembling tents. Some Polish women work as household servants—slaves more precisely—for the Nazi homes, and now, it seems, in the homes of Army officers. Caterine says she will have nothing to do with this. If one of those poor women were to come here, she would immediately pack and move out. Fred asked innocently, "what if they just wanted to use the toilet?" Caterine glared but did not reply. Merry Christmas!

December 25, 1939

Christmas Day. There was excitement in our home with a dressed tree and gaily wrapped presents beneath it. I had placed my order for the wrapping paper in advance, to einsure that it would arrive on time. Some of the presents were obtained by barter (Resi), with cigarettes used as the coin of the realm.

Elisabet is home for a few days. Paul, too. He does not say where he is stationed, but his batman has shown us a few post cards from Wiesbaden in Hesse, Germany.

Paul, Caterine and Fred went off to Kaiser Wilhelm Memorial Church for services; and Elisabet and I to a small French Protestant church with declining congregants in the eastern part of the city. The chapel was built at the time of Frederick the Great, whose court spoke French. The structure was constructed of weathered granite and overgrown by unmanageable ivy.

The pastor was an old man, but at times his voice soared to the rafters as he described man's eternal battle with evil. Nothing specific. Services were in French.

After, the pastor greeted the congregants as they left the chapel. Elisabet brought me around the back of the church to a path leading deep into the old cemetery. She took me to the end of the burial ground and pointed to a site next to an old linden tree.

"I pray God will spare us both," she whispered. "But if He takes me first, this is where I want to be buried." She pointed to the Linden tree. I could barely hear her, but felt goose pimples on my arms. This strange talk was upsetting.

The scene receded into consciousness, superseded by a blurry vignette. I saw the interior of our comfortable living room on father's birthday! Mother was seated at our piano, and I stood beside her, My tutor had taught me the words to *The Linden Tree*, my father's favorite, and I had practiced it all week long. When I finished the song, my father took me in his arms, and I saw a tear running down his cheek. I never learned why the song affected him so.

"They want to lock up," I heard Elisabet saying. "Let's go before they lock us out."

December 26, 1939

Disastrous news. The von Manigs have been informed that Fred must join the junior Hitler Youth. The main reasons for sending him to Mrs. Robinson's was to shield him from the Nazi rot. This has put a damper on our New

Year's festivities. It may mean taking him out of Mrs. Robinson's and enrolling him in the local schools.

With Caterine's permission, I showed the letter to Mosby, and he brought it to the Bradfords. As expected, Duncan shrugged his shoulders and handed the letter to Kirstin, who read it carefully. She copied down Fred's name, and the particulars, which I supplied.

She asked to keep the letter. Why not? Nothing I can do with it.

January 3, 1940

The chief of the American Diplomatic legation and his staff are invited to the annual New Year's reception at the German Foreign Ministry, one of the few official functions that the American Embassy still attends.. This means formal dress for everyone and dress uniform and sword for me, which I shall wear for the first time. The Bradfords are going, of course, but Mosby and wife will remain in the embassy, since both men are seldom absent at the same time..

We checked our coats, but only the Bradfords were required to stand on the receiving line. With a sweep of his hand, he introduced "his staff" and was moved along to the next receiver. To no one's surprise, Reich Minister Joachim Ribbentrop was not present to greet the guests. He had the same "urgent business" excuse last year, but the guests were assured that he will try to join them later.

The reception had a huge turnout. Servants circulated with trays held shoulder-high, offering refreshment, but servants were few, and most of the guests waited with ill-concealed impatience. All were in formal dress, with the attendant glitter. A familiar scene: Uniforms with rows of medals, ladies with colorful bands of silk diagonally across their bountiful chests, signifying various kinds of royal orders. The American contingent clustered on the right side of the room.

I tried conversing with a trio of young ladies, two of whom I had met at one of the embassy parties, but the noise level in the hall was frustrating, and they spoke only Spanish.

At the end of the hall was a huge marble staircase leading up to the first floor. A discrete sign directed the way to the toilettes. two husky guards, dressed in some kind of diplomatic livery, were stationed on each side of the stairs. Actually, I had no need to visit the facilities, but was anxious to get away, so I started up the stairs, with my sword knocking against my leg. Halfway up the stairs, I turned around to search the hall for Elisabet; but she was lost in that seething mass.

I saw Kirstin Bradford ease her way to the side of the hall, where three men were standing, dressed in navy blue uniforms with gold bands around their sleeves. One of them, a gray-haired gentleman of medium height, kissed her hand. His sleeve had a broad band, so I assumed that he was the ranking officer. A closer look told me he was Canaris, the Abwehr man I had met at the Heydrichs. He gathered her aside, and the two conversed alone for a few minutes. She then opened her purse and handed him a folded letter, which he slipped into his pocket. They chatted further, until the two officers rejoined them, and she walked away.

By the time I returned to our party, it was time to go.

January 5, 1940

A joyful Caterine joined me for breakfast this morning. Last evening she received a late telephone call informing her that Fred need not leave Mrs. Robinson. The previous order has been rescinded!!

Later at the embassy, I gave the ecstatic news to Kirstin, along with my effusive thanks, but she hardly acknowledged it. What, if any, is her relationship to Canaris—the head of the German Abwehr, for God's sake? So much seems to be passing me by.

Arvid Carlsson, the Swede, invited me after the attachés' meeting to join him in the public room of the Golden Hindr. Strange, he knows I don't drink but invited me anyway. Arvid is a likable fellow who spent two years in the United States at the agricultural college at Cornell University and speaks fluent American-English. Tonight, he appeared tipsy or at least wanted me to think so.

He told me about the 13 German Pz II's and III's, and one Pz IV given to the Finnish army by the Nazis. This information he was about to relate was collected by the Swedish officers serving as "observers."

The Finns had experienced great difficulty with the tanks in the sub-zero weather: battery trouble—the acid froze and batteries cracked; gasket trouble—the rubber cracked and leaks appeared; engine trouble—engines would not turn over in the cold, and so on. He had a long list, and made no objection when I copied down the particulars.

My impression was that Carlsson had been instructed to furnish me the information, but to ensure that the transfer could not be construed as official. Afterward, I went back to the embassy and woke up Mosby. He watched me type up the report and sent it out that night.

February 5, 1940

The Finnish war is over. The Finns are in full retreat and the Finnish leader, von Mannheim, has asked for terms. Helsinki is forced to accept the loss of the Karelia Peninsula, so that

Leningrad can be protected. From whom? Surely not from the Germans—their friendly ally.

April 7, 1940

"The game's afoot," as Sherlock Holmes would say. When I walked past the Danau, the lion was standing. Sure enough, there was a message.

Germany will invade Norway tomorrow! No surprise to the attachés, who have been expecting an invasion. Britain has already landed troops at Narvik in Northern Norway, Narvik being the harbor from which the Swedish iron ore was being exported to Germany. With Narvik in British hands, German iron imports would be fatally interrupted.

The information was immediately sent on its way to the States. The fact that the alert came so close to the time of the German invasion means that the German order was a spur-of-the-moment response to the original British order to capture Narvik.

April 8, 1940

Another "heads up" from our benefactor at the
Danau. "Germany will invade Denmark on
April 9th." Denmark has no standing army, and
no military attachés, so that the German
occupation will be swift. For the embassy
people, this means that we will be cut off from
our source of supplies in Denmark and will
have to rely solely on Portugal or Sears
Roebuck.

April 21,1940

According to the loudspeakers, the German
Army has occupied all of Norway and chased
the British out of Narvik. Also, a British aircraft
carrier has been sunk. The German invasion
comes as no surprise to the attachés. One of
them bought in a photograph of some captured
British soldiers dressed in summer uniforms,
standing against a background of snow!

The German Amy has a language advantage in
that many of the German soldiers speak
Norwegian. They had been taken into
Norwegian homes as children after the Great
War "to fatten them up." There, they learned

the language, which was to later prove a convenience for the German occupation.

Everyone wonders when the land war with France and Britain will begin? The conventional wisdom is that Germany will use the old von Schlieffen plan with a bold thrust trough Belgium.

One thing bothers me. Paul, who now commands an armored brigade, sends post cards to us from Wiesbaden, which is a long way from the plains of Belgium. When I look at the map, I see that the nearest way from Wiesbaden into France is through Luxembourg and the Ardennes Forest.

When I mentioned the Ardennes Forest to the attachés, they scoffed: too impenetrable, not suitable for vehicular traffic (let alone tanks). Yet I recall that the previous Portuguese attaché, Renato Caravalho, said that he spent a week at St. Vith in the Ardennes region on his honeymoon. I also remember that he said that there were roads through the forest, large enough to accommodate big lumber trucks.

Also, if it means anything, the road maps of Luxembourg have been sold out at the Mittlekamp Book Store.

Putting it all together, I wonder if the Germans might thrust west through Luxembourg and the Ardennes. Should I send my speculations to my bosses in Washington? Mosby says I should. I hope it doesn't backfire on me.

May 1, 1940

News from the Danau Konditorei. "Germany will invade Belgium, Netherlands and Luxembourg on May 10th." We all knew from the newspapers and the loudspeakers, that invasion was imminent, but now we know the date. The information was, of course, sent off post haste to Washington.

A thrust through Luxembourg! This confirms my speculation. I hope General Moore is taking note of my communications, if, in fact, he is still around.

May 11, 1940

The war in the west has begun with a sudden drive into Netherlands and Belgium, and, simultaneously, a Panzer thrust into the Ardennes. Since the attachés remember that I had been asking questions about the Ardennes, I am now credited with remarkable insight.

May 24, 1940

Near as I can determine from the newsreels, Army Guderian still has a majority of light tanks but an increasing number of mediums, of which there are at present only 200 Pz IV's. The French, too, have an excellent tank, the Char B1-15 (Heavy), but, like the Polish 7tp, few tank units of battalion size and most of those are scattered among the infantry, just as we did (or still do?) in the U.S.. In fact, the allies have 4,000 tanks compared to only 2,000 for the Germans, but the French tanks are scattered, while the Germans have independent tank units that move, MOVE, MOVE!

June 5, 1940

The German army has made tremendous gains, especially the panzer corps led by General Heinz Guderian. Also, I keep reading about the Panzer brigade of that Erwin Rommel, the Nazi author who wrote the autobiography about the infantry in the Great War. Like Paul, he has changed over to panzers.

Some think that the Panzers will turn south and isolate Paris, as in the old von Schlieffen plan, but I suspect (another of my hunches) that they will turn north and isolate the British troops along the coast. More dramatic. Something Hitler would like. This would virtually end the war and compel the surrender of France.

Mosby insists that I write up my suspicions and send them in. Any day now, I expect a blast from Washington. That fellow Mosby is going to get me into big trouble.

June 6, 1940

The Allied Expeditionary Force, without its vehicles, tanks, armaments or even rifles, is back in Britain after a hair-raising retreat across the English Channel. Only one division (Canadian, according to the German newspapers) is completely armed. What can Britain do now? A new prime minister, Winston Churchill of Gallipoli notoriety, is back, to lead the British people. Into what? According to Berlin newspapers, the British upper class secretly admire Hitler and vow that they can work with him.

June 10, 1940

Italy has declared war on the Allies. The junior attaché, Major Mario Carolini, seems embarrassed when we mention this to him.

June 14, 1940

Berlin is delirious in its welcome for her victorious heroes. It is almost unsafe to go out onto Pariser Square, for fear of being trampled by the jubilant crowd. Paul is home on leave. He is withdrawn and sits staring at the Berlin newspapers, without reading them. We do not question him—or at least, I don't. What he tells Caterine, I'm sure I don't know.

Everyone asks how long will it be before Britain comes to terms? Hitler is so patient, they say. He has offered Britain such generous terms, and yet they refuse. Well, it's on their head.

The public is convinced that Adolph Hitler is a military genius. Victory in 4 weeks! Germany could not do the same in 4 years of the Great War!

June 16, 1940

Berlin is flooded with French wine and cheese. Ration cards are unnecessary—as long as the feast lasts. Women wear silk stockings with a Boulevard Haussmann (Paris) label.

June 17, 1940

The Soviets have seized Buchavina and Bessarabia from Romania. This puts them perilously close to Ploesti in Rumania, the source of Hitler's oil supply. This seems to me an important development—a very important development, to which few of us give adequate attention. I made a note of this and sent it in.

July 2, 1940

At the attachés' meeting yesterday, Arvid
Carlsson showed me a newspaper
advertisement for a new, full-length feature
film called *Campaign in France*. I met him late
afternoon. We took the underground and
walked a few blocks to the cinema. It was in a
rather run-down part of the city with dreary
tenement houses. We lined up for tickets for the
6 pm showing. Most in the ticket line were
teen-aged kids. Those dressed in their Hitler
Youth or the Hitler maiden uniforms were
admitted free.

The movie exceeded my wildest expectations.
A compilation of newsreels, it showed an
armored column advancing, halting, fighting,
battling, repairing breakdowns, fighting enemy
aircraft, etc. Rehearsed scenes were kept to a
minimum. The movie was all I could have
hoped for, and more.

After the film was over, I persuaded Carlsson to
see the film again, and we lined up for tickets.
The second showing was even more productive.
Many of the vehicles which had escaped my
notice the first time were now recognizable. I

resolved to see the film again tomorrow and bring my notebook with me.

One thing was noticeable. The number of medium tanks (Pz IV's) had considerably increased. Also, the 88mm aircraft gun was being used as a tank destroyer, but this was old hat, since we had known that already.

July 6, 1940

I spent the last week polishing my notes. I further identified the vehicles and more fully described the horse-drawn units, which have not gotten any smaller.

I also made a few observations.

1. The effectiveness of the armored column did not depend exclusively on the tanks, nor on the anti-tank guns, but on the Ju 87 ("Stuka") dive bombers, with their 300-pound bombs ("flying artillery"); and on the Me 109 fighter planes, which protect the Stukas, and permit them to fly unchallenged.

2. Any distinct tank advance means that the horse-drawn support units (as well as the

bicycle, motorcycle, etc.) will lag far behind, leaving the front and rear vulnerable.

3. Any attack on the German armored column will have the best opportunity for success if launched against the flank at the junction of armor and support.

4. An attack on the support column would be highly profitable, since that part has little defense, apart from the horse-drawn 88's and the infantry.

5. The medium tank (Pz IV) has inherent maintenance troubles, and most cannot be repaired in situ, but must be abandoned or towed back to a repair center

6. INVINCIBILITY OF THE NAZI PANZER COLUMN IS LARGELY EXAGGERATION, AND WITH PROPER PREPARATION AND LEADERSHIP, THE U.S .CAN EASILY MATCH OR BETTER THEM.

I drew the above, and a few other conclusions and Mosby forwarded them. Is anybody reading this stuff?

August 6, 1940

While in the canteen, I received a telephone call from someone who called himself "Genomi," asking me to meet him at 8 pm in a nearby park. The caller sounded like Edvard Karbis, the friend of Mr. Genomi. But why the subterfuge? Was he in trouble?

Indeed he was. Big trouble. Orders had gone out for his arrest in what Berliner's call a *nacht und nebel* (night and fog) operation. Fortunately, he was not home when the SS showed up, and his 16-year-old daughter, Magda, was at a Hitler Maidens meeting.

He told me that his only hope was to escape to Prague, where he and his daughter could be hidden away by friends. Could I help them?

Help them? What could I do? And yet, this is a man whom my honored friend and benefactor Mr. Genomi would lay down his life for. Where was his daughter? He put his fingers to his mouth and whistled. A scared 16-year-old girl in Hitler Maiden's uniform emerged from behind some bushes. When I asked if they had a place to spend the night, he shook his head.

Good God! It was up to me. I was their last hope.

I took them home with me by street car and led them through the cellar entrance and up the stairs to the main floor. A quick look around assured me that we had not been detected. Caterine, Fred and Elisabet were seated at a table playing a game and the Geulens were in the kitchen. Up the main stairs to the first (European) floor we crept. I pointed out the toilet and led them to a vacant room. It was rather dusty but not intolerably so.

They gave me their identification papers. What were they going to do for food? Sorry, they will have to go hungry for the rest of the day. I promised to return tomorrow, as early as I could, with something to eat.

August 7, 1940

I left the house early to avoid questions. As soon as Bradford was up and about, I laid the matter before him. He said nothing, but referred me to Kirstin. She examined the documents, and we waited for Mosby to return from his morning duties. When he got back, they talked together for several minutes, and then she left.

Mosby asked me why I wanted to help them. I explained what Mr. Genomi meant to me and my deep obligation to assist his friend. He seemed to accept this and told me to come back late afternoon. With that, he disappeared into the mystery room.

As instructed, I returned at 6 pm. Jean answered the knock and announced my arrival to Mosby inside the mystery room. He told me to come back in a half hour. I picked up the Berlin newspaper and read the story about Hitler's great plans for a new and more beautiful Berlin.

An hour later Mosby emerged, and I caught a glimpse of the mystery room. It was filled with files, photographic equipment and a small printing press. Rather curious paraphernalia for a Marine captain, yes?

"Got it!" he said and handed me some papers. First item was a letter of authorization written by someone supposed to be in the Gestapo, on the behalf of Edvard Kubis and his daughter, Magda. The letter looked absolutely authentic, down to the paper and the seal. In addition, there were other documents, including an authorization signed by Heydrich himself, instructing Kubis to open a fencing *saal* in Prague for German officers.

Moby gave me careful instructions. A reservation in second class has been made for my friend and his daughter tomorrow on the 0930 train to Prague. He must not appear timid. If challenged, he is to show the Heydrich letter. Above all, he must disappear when he reaches Prague, never to show his face in public. Mosby will instruct Vincent to have the limousine at my house at 0850. Be ready.

It was dark when I got home. I crept up the stairs, confident that I had not been noticed.

Kubis and Magda were just finishing a meal. I was told that Mrs. Geulen had brought it. And had laundered their clothes—my partner in crime.

August 8, 1940

Vincent showed up at the precise hour. Kubis and his daughter were waiting at the curb. I walked to the vehicle and Resi Geulen came with me.

Magda kissed Resi, and Kubis shook my hand, without saying a word. Last we saw of them they were on the way to the station. Later, I tried to thank Mosby, but he shrugged his shoulders and turned away. Where do we get men like these?

August 10, 1940

Elisabet has been gone for more than a week now. Her latest assignment is the city of Porto in Portugal, to replace the incumbent consul who has been recalled. She has been trained in the Portuguese language by the Foreign Affairs Ministry, so can fit right into the office without difficulty.

I miss her terribly.

August 15, 1940

An urgent call from Caterine. Fred was very ill. I rushed home and found the boy lying on the living room sofa, groaning and clutching his abdomen. Mrs. Geulen was mopping his brow.

He had had pain since morning and hadn't gone to class. When Caterine called the hospital, she was told that since the boy was a military dependent, he has to go to an Army hospital 12 kilometers away.

I immediately telephoned Felix at his home. Morgan answered, and I hurriedly explained the situation. She gave me the extension number at the Charite Hospital, where Felix could be reached.

He answered promptly—Thank God!—and I explained the situation. He told me that Fred has to come to the hospital immediately and that he would send an ambulance. But the boy will have to come as a private patient. I assured him that I would be responsible.

A half hour later an ambulance drew up to the house and Fred was carefully loaded into it. Caterine and I rode with him. The boy was taken to an examining room on an old rickety stretcher, and Felix joined us.

He explained that Fred has been admitted to the service of a Dr. Heinz Forester. Professor Privy Counselor Dr. Ernst Ferdinand Sauerbruch, the reigning prince, was away at an international meeting, along with two other members of the staff, leaving one of his other assistants in charge. But Felix did not recommend him, so he admitted the patient to Dr. Forester's service. He added that we may find him somewhat peculiar in his ways, but if ever Felix needed an operation, Forester would be the one who would do it.

Dr. Forester came into the room and studied the lab reports. He was a thin, dark-haired man with a thoughtful manner that conveyed confidence. He examined Fred, pressing his finger on a point in the abdomen that made Fred cry out in pain. Forester ordered the boy brought into the operating room and told Caterine that a local anesthetic would be used. The boy will not be asleep, but he will feel no pain.

Fred was wheeled out of the room and the surgeons left, leaving Corrine and me seated on a well-worn bench. I assured her again of my absolute confidence in Felix's recommendations.

It seemed no more than a half hour (but of course it was longer) that the surgeon and Felix came back into the room and showed us a small jar with an inflamed, pus-filled appendix floating in the formaldehyde. Yes, we can talk to the boy after they tidy up his bed. The mother can remain with him during the night, provided that the head nurse gives her approval, which she will.

August 25, 1940

Berlin had its first night bomber raid. The British use their twin-engine bombers, the Handly Page Halifax or the Avro Manchester, but they carry only light bombs, so the damage was slight. On the other hand, the bombers sustained considerable losses.

September 7, 1940

Big news. Congress has voted the first peacetime draft. The goal is 1,200,000 men under arms. What an opportunity for an available Army officer!

Also, the president has swapped 50 old World War destroyers for rights to a series of islands from Newfoundland to British Guyana.

September 10, 1940

Another night air raid. Reichstag hit (no one injured) and, believe it or not, a bomb fell in the garden of the American Embassy (no one injured). We had just put large letters spelling "USA" on the roof of the embassy.

November 8, 1940

News of the US election. Roosevelt has won a third term. The German newspapers have been following the campaign quite closely, and guess whom they have been rooting for?

Here at the embassy, Willkie was the favorite with the regular State Department employees, not that anyone here was able to vote. I needn't ask Mosby for his choice, since his photograph of FDR speaks for itself.

Well, at least we have continuity of command.

November 10, 1940

The air war against Britain has commenced. The newsreels show scenes of German Condor bombers sinking British merchant vessels in the English Channel, and describe the great damage done to British infrastructure. Also, we see the smiling faces of the young German pilots emerging from their planes at the conclusion of their air raids. According to the newspapers, the British cannot withstand the aerial destruction and must accept terms.

November 12, 1940

The air war against Britain continues. So far, the RAF seem to be putting up a good fight, but their losses, according to the official German Luftwaffe communiqués, have been staggering. Any day now, the war will be over.

During the night the RAF sent another bomber formation over Berlin! It did little damage, thanks to the 88's and 105 Howies ringing the city, but it made Goering's boast seem hollow: "If any plane ever gets through, you can call me 'Meier'" (dunce).

The upshot of the raid is that the block officer has compelled all residents, at the first notice of a raid, to report to an air raid shelter. Our shelter is in the basement of the home next door.

January 4, 1941

We hear talk about an impending invasion of Britain. The stories confuse me. Paul is home on leave. He wears the Iron cross with the Tank Combat Clasp. Would he be given leave if an invasion of Britain were pending? Might Hitler's plans of invasion be a bluff? Would he risk an invasion without absolute air supremacy? And so far, the RAF is still very much in the air.

But who am I to judge? Anyway, Mosby advised me to forward my suspicions to General Moore, in the CO's office.

February 8, 1941

Elisabet has returned from Portugal and is back at the Foreign Affairs Ministry. Among her new duties, she will be a substitute courier (whatever that entails). I feel so abandoned when she is away.

Another air raid. The British twin engines remain over the city for only a few minutes, and apart from disturbing our sleep, they do little damage.

February 10, 1941

Elisabet told Caterine that the regular courier is ill and that she must take his place until he returns to duty. She has left by train for Switzerland.

I have acquired (with great difficulty) a gold wedding ring and had the words "Love is Eternal" engraved on the inside. Elisabet has agreed to wear it, but on the right ring finger, to forestall questions. Many women here wear a single band on the left ring finger for betrothal and two bands for marriage.

Mosby is often gone all night. He leaves the embassy at dusk wearing workman's clothing; and returns in the early hours. What is he doing? I presume that he has Bradford's approval, and that whatever he does, is in the best interests of the United States. During the day, he spends much time in the mystery room, as well as in the consular section, dressed in civilian clothing, speaking with the hapless supplicants.

This afternoon, as he was leaving the mystery room holding a waste basket filled with papers to be destroyed, Jean asked him to change a light bulb. He set down the basket and followed her into the kitchen.

Quickly, I rushed to the waste basket and picked up a paper. It had an unfamiliar coat of arms and was written in Spanish. Although I couldn't be sure, it appeared to be a visa for El Salvador, in Central America. The paper was not uniformly inked, so it might be an early run. I put it back and returned to my seat, just as Mosby re-entered the room to retrieve the basket.

Does this mean that he is making and distributing counterfeit visas?

April 3, 1941

The lion was standing today. I fetched the message and brought it to the embassy. The message reads: "Germany will invade Yugoslavia and Greece on April 6th."

Yugoslavia has recently changed governments and the present one is favorable to the Allied cause. Greece, likewise, has a pro-British government—at the moment.

Could this change in the Yugo and Greek governments presage a German invasion? I brought this up at the attaché meeting, without disclosing the details. Naturally, the Greek and Yugo attaches were especially disturbed by the discussion, since it was their homelands that were being threatened.

What would Germany gain from these invasions (besides gold)? Protection against a British invasion? Surely there was no danger of Britain invading southeast Europe, since Britain is hard put to defend its own country. What then? The answer, I suspect, is that Germany plans to invade the Soviet Union and does not want an undefended flank. What other reason can there be?

Hitler gets most of his oil from the Ploesti Oil Fields in Rumania. This source must be secured, if his army is to operate. The Soviets are already close by in Bessarabia and North Buchavina, 150 miles from Ploesti.

A few of the attachés have come to the same conclusion, but if Hitler does intend to invade the Soviet Union, he had best do it soon, so that his Army would not be interrupted by the unforgiving Russian winter.

April 14, 1941

Helen caught me reading the *Frankfurter Algemeine Zeitung* with my feet up on my desk. Mr. Bradford wants to see me right away! I straightened my tie and hurried to his apartment. He and Mosby were examining a yellow paper from communications.

Bradford handed me the uncoded message marked "secret." It was sent by Alan Dulles, the OSS agent in Bern, Switzerland, requesting information about Elisabet de Talligny, a Berlin resident and employee of the German Foreign Ministry.

Bradford confirmed that my fiancée is the party in question. He ordered me to write a small biographical sketch to be sent to Bern. Warning bells sounded.

Any chances of my reply being intercepted? A small chance, but it can't be dismissed. In which case, I argued, the young lady is as good as dead—as well as her family. If she is assisting us, we have a obligation to protect her.

Do I know an alternative?

Yes, I could go to Bern and speak with Mr. Dulles myself. No written record.

Bradford glanced at Moby who nodded. There was a late afternoon flight, and Helen made the arrangements. And so, I found myself on a Lufthansa flight to Bern, my very first passenger plane ride. Anyone who has ever flown over the Alps, buffeted by the winds and thermal drafts, will know how uncomfortable the flight can be.

I went through customs and officialdom, and was greeted by a familiar face. It was that of Lloyd Sutton, whom I had not seen since the Hanover. I rushed over and warmly shook his hand. State had transferred him here from Dundee, and he was now Alan Dulles' assistant and bodyguard, with a full consul's rating (temporary).

On the way to Dulles' office, Lloyd brought me up to date. He and Cornelia were married in Dundee, Scotland, and she found work in the consular office (with a little help from Dad). By the time Lloyd received orders to Switzerland, she was 5 months pregnant, so he sent her home, uncertain of what lay ahead.

What brings me to Bern? I explained to him the dispatch we had received, told him about Elisabet, and why I did not want to answer his query in writing. He conceded that there was always a small chance of dispatches being intercepted. He then went on to bring me up to date on what was happening in Bern.

A weird story. Alan Dulles was an officer in the Office of Strategic Services, the American counterpart of the British M-6. He had been sent to Switzerland in the hope that he could latch on to some valuable secret information. Until 3 months ago, his mission had had little tangible value. True, there were numerous visits from Rhine River barge captains, railroad workers, aircraft personnel, each with "vital" information about this or that, and each expecting considerable remuneration. The information they supplied was superficial, contradictory, and in fact valueless, although a considerable sum of American dollars had changed hands. Likewise, the German expatriates, the Swiss businessmen and the foreign travelers who had just come from Germany. All valueless, all costly.

Then one day a little German man wearing a dark suit and a white shirt with a wing collar showed up in Bern. Who he was and where he came from are unknown. He first tried to meet the British consul but was refused an appointment; and then tried to see Dulles, who turned him away. Dulles feared the man might be an agent provocateur sent by the Swiss government as an excuse to shut us down.

He continued the story. Instead of returning to Germany, the man contacted a German friend who was living in Berne. The friend was a personal acquaintance of Alan, whom he persuaded to see the fellow.

The courier appeared, delivered the contents of his satchel, refused to accept money, and departed. No names, no explanations, nothing.

The documents left by the man consisted of 200-300 dispatches and orders, sent by the German Foreign Ministry. They were in no chronologic order. Some of the papers were timely, some predictive, but all interesting. Even the out-of-date papers had value, for they gave insight into how the German government reasoned. They had never seen anything like this before.

Was the material authentic or a hoax? Of course, it was rushed to Washington, and the retuned message instructed Dulles to maintain close contact with the courier.

The man showed up 3 weeks later with another batch of papers. By then, Lloyd had arrived. They treated the courier with kid gloves, but he refused all compensation—not even a glass of cognac. Nor did they even learn his name. Lloyd tried to trail him, but he vanished into the night.

A month ago, another courier appeared. This time it was a woman—an attractive woman in her late twenties. She left a considerable stack of German Foreign Office cables and left the office. Lloyd followed her to the airport and watched her board the plane. After she departed, he obtained, with the help of a handsome gratuity, the name as it appeared in her passport, "Elisabet de Talligny," and now his friend tells him he is in love with her.

Lloyd bought me in to see Alan Dulles. He listened as I explained my reason for coming in person to Bern and what I knew of Elisabet. The truth is I knew precious little about the political opinions of her or her family, but I knew the reason why Fred attended Mrs. Robinson's school and the fact that Paul von Manig is a poorly paid German general.

April 18, 1941

This evening, after an early supper in the canteen, I was sitting in my office when Mr. Bradford walked in. This was the first time he did this. Usually, he sends Helen to fetch me.

He said that he was going for a walk around the grounds and asked if I would join him. He has been known to walk outdoors to avoid the risk of having an important conversation picked up by some unknown electronic intercept.

Curious. We stopped near an old beech tree. After assuring himself that we could not be overheard, he told me that he had in mind, for me, a very dangerous mission. Thus far, Mosby has been handling this matter himself, but if something were to happen to him, an instant replacement would be required. Do I want the job?

I thought of the Mosby family without a husband and father. If Dwaine has taken the risk, what possible excuse could I have? I told him I was ready.

He explained that tomorrow, I was to be at 0950 at the underground (subway) entrance four blocks from the embassy. Mosby also will be standing there. At exactly 1000 we were both to cross over to a nearby tram stop and wait. A covered truck will come by and pick us up. We are to climb in quickly and remain quiet. The truck people will be studying us carefully, as they go about their work. They know Mosby; it will be me who receives most of their attention.

When the trip is finished, we will be brought back to the tram station. Mosby will return to the embassy; I can go home. Tomorrow, if he is satisfied with my performance, Mosby will explain to me what is going on,

April 19, 1941

Waited impatiently for the appointed hour. At five minutes before 10 am, I met Mosby at the entrance to the subway and crossed to the tram stop. Mosby was dressed in his usual overalls outfit; I was in slacks and open collar shirt, with my sleeves rolled up. At 10 o'clock a truck pulled up. Mosby quickly climbed up, and I followed, but a pair of hands were needed to pull me in. Apart from occasional light coming through the canvas flap at the rear of the truck, the interior of the cab was dark.

We rode in the darkness for fifteen minutes and then came to a stop in what smelled like the petrochemical district. Someone lit a lamp, and I looked around. Besides Mosby and myself, there were the driver and two other men, both dressed in workmen's clothing, one of whom sat at a radio transmitter.

The equipment was quickly readied, and a paper handed to the operator. At the exact minute, determined by a pocket watch, a lengthy message was sent by telegraph keys. The paper was then handed to Mosby, the light extinguished, and the truck began moving. We were let off at the tram station, and the truck drove away. Mosby and I then parted company.

April 19, 1941

I had no opportunity to talk to either Bradford or Mosby until noontime, when Mosby took me for a walk on the embassy grounds.

What he told me was astonishing.

In the old days, Berlin had a large Communist following, which all but disappeared, when the Nazis came to power. Not entirely, since an espionage network still remained, which, although small, was the only known anti-Nazi organization still in operation in Berlin.

Now for the astounding part. This anti-Nazi network also includes some person or persons who have access to the minutes of the German General Staff! The cell periodically transmits reports to Moscow. A few weeks ago, the cell, which some call "the Red Orchestra," began to make their information available also to the United States. This may have been the decision of some of the cell members, not all of whom are communists; or it may have come from the Soviet High Command (acting without Stalin's knowledge). Despite the non-aggression pact with Germany, the Soviet high command still had lingering fears of a Nazis invasion.

Mosby's job was to ensure a steady flow of information from Berlin to Washington. Were he "eliminated," someone else (me) must be instantly ready to replace him.

Neither Bradford nor Mosby had ever discussed with me the contents of the message handed to Mosby by the "Red Orchestra."

April 25, 1941

Another air raid. Bombs fell near the zoo and gave the elephants a fright.

May 20, 1941

Caterine and Fred are spending the week end in Rudorf, a few stations away from Berlin by local train. The von Manigs have a small hunting cottage in the Arnholtz Forest, with well water and kerosene lanterns.

Elisabet and I have the whole two days together. I came home Friday night, and she greeted me wearing a low-cut evening gown. We had a wonderful candlelight dinner, after which we danced away the evening, before retiring to my quarters. Elizabet replaced the gold band from the right to the left ring finger; and we fell into each other's arms. As I felt this heavenly creature in my embrace, my love swelled up inside me, so that I had difficulty talking.

The night passed blissfully. We sunk into a deep slumber with her arm resting across my chest.

May 21, 1941

Morning, we heard a soft rap on the door and Resi Geulen walked in with a tray of coffee and biscuits. She set it down on the night table and left. Neither of us had any desire to get up, so we remained in bed the entire day, resolving to spend Sunday morning in bed as well.

June 15, 1941

The lion again. The message: "Hitler will begin his invasion of the Soviet Union on June 22, 1941." Thus far, the campaign against the Yugos and the Greeks has gone almost flawlessly, according to the official German army communiqués, and the Rumanian and Hungarian governments are now firmly in the Nazi orbit, so that Hitler's southeast flank is secure, and the road is now clear for a Soviet invasion.

June 22, 1941

Germany has begun its colossal invasion of the Soviet Union with 2 million soldiers. Further, the attack was begun without a preliminary artillery bombardment. Straight in, without warning. The instructors at the American War College would probably give the German generals a failing grade for disregarding a well-established military principle, but I doubt it will much trouble General Heinz Guderian, the German tank commander.

Russia has the largest army in Europe and the largest number of tanks. The quality of both will soon be tested, but the attachés have little expectation that Hitler can be stopped. One thing bothers me. In the brief newsreel clips I saw of the Soviet tanks rolling through Red Square in Moscow, the tanks had no antennas. Do they lack the communication capability of the German tanks?

August 19, 1941

The Nazis have had two months of unbelievable success. Whole Soviet armies have been captured. Minsk, Smolensk and Kiev have fallen! The Germans seem to have three armies in motion: the Northern, which has Leningrad under siege; the Central, directed toward Moscow; and the Southern, heading for the Caucasus (oil). So far, so good for the Nazis.

The German newspapers report the capture of a million Soviet prisoners. What will they do with them? Berlin is filled with bedraggled gangs of Russian men under armed guard, either at work, or on the way to work. If you get too near to them, the guards point their rifles at you. The men smell horribly, as one might expect, since they are without hygienic facilities.

The attachés whisper about executions in Poland, but the stories are too horrible to be believed. (When I mentioned it to Mosby, he replied, "Believe it!")

August 31, 1941

Another night raid by the RAF with minimal bomb damage. Our nocturnal bomb shelter is in the basement of our next-door neighbor, a retired doll manufacturer with a plant in Spandau, now making gas masks.

October 13, 1941

At the attaché meeting, Colonel Ramon del Aguila, the Spanish attaché, told us that some fellow officers in the Spanish Blue Division have written that they were compelled to cease mobile operations with the onset of the muddy season, when their Pz III tanks get irretrievably stuck in the mud.

November 1, 1941

Our communication bulletin reports that an American destroyer, the USS Reuben James, has been sunk by a German submarine with a loss of 150 men. This is the third instance of an attack on American shipping.

Item. The US has extended to the Soviets 1 billion dollars in credit. I hope we don't expect to get any of it back soon.

November 11, 1941

My precious is in Italy on courier duty. Would that I was with her! Perhaps we could find some old priest who would perform the wedding rites. Sure, and maybe Mussolini himself would do it.

November 24, 1941

Winter has come to the Soviet Union with a vengeance, and the consensus is that the German troops are ill-prepared for snow. According to the Hungarian attaché, the German soldiers have no winter clothing (yet).

Every few days there is a new collection drive: gold rings, metals, pots, pans and now, warm clothing. When they came to our door, Mrs. Geulen gave them an ancient fur coat that had once belonged to Caterine.

Elisabet has returned from Rome and has brought back an Italian salami and goat cheese. Tomorrow, she leaves for Switzerland by train.

December 1, 1941

We attachés have an abundance of information about conditions on the eastern front. Hungary, Rumania, Italy and Spain all have troops fighting with the Germans in the Soviet Union, and all have accredited attachés. The Hungarian attaché, Colonel Jozsef Kodaly, has been especially informative. The German's battle plans called for a quick campaign, lasting no more than 3 months, with no provision made for extending the operation. Is it possible that the German General Staff could have been so improvident as to fail to make allowances for winter? I forgot. Hitler is in charge of the operation.

We never tire of gossip. Some say that Admiral Canaris is back in favor. According to them, Canaris had warned Hitler that the German Secret Service had no reliable information about the Soviet reserves in the east beyond the Carpathians, and until that information can be obtained, the invasion should be delayed.

Hitler ignored that advice, and now, after standing in the dunce's corner for 6 months, Canaris is back in favor.

December 2, 1941

Paul has requested a heavy sweater. I contributed my thick woolen pullover that performed well in Utah, where the temperature can plunge to 30 below (Fahrenheit). Unfortunately, it has the word "Army" printed on the front, but perhaps he can wear it inside out.

Mosby has obtained an important bit of information from the Red Orchestra. They told him that the German High Staff has learned from their agent in Tokyo, that Japan will not attack the Soviet Union, but instead, will advance south into the British, French, American and Dutch territories. The Soviets can now reassign their 30 fully-equipped eastern divisions for service on the Moscow front. Their T-34 tanks have a wide track, which they claim can easily outperform the Pz IV in winter.

Captain Carlsson (Sweden), who is regarded as our authority on cold weather equipment, told us that the German motor oil will freeze in cold temperatures and that the tank engine (gasoline) of the Pz III and IV cannot be started unless you build a fire under it, which is unsafe. The Soviets keep their tanks (diesel) running through the night, as well they might, since they have an abundant fuel supply.

Also, I learned that the Soviets are not as unknowledgeable about tanks as I supposed. During the Weimar Republic days, when German tanks were forbidden by the Versailles Treaty, the Germans had a clandestine tank school at Kazan, Soviet Union, for 6 years, which they shared with the Russians. Both countries tested various tank models. It was here the Russians first developed the BT series tanks, which incorporated Christie's ideas.

Also, further gossip from the attachés. Stalin has brought back General Zukov, whom he had earlier dismissed after the fall of Kiev. Zukov, the attachés say, has a particular talent for deploying tanks, and so he may yet come to the rescue of Moscow.

Elisabet's return is long overdue. She was supposed to have arrived yesterday. Caterine was immediately concerned. I cannot sleep from worrying.

December 5, 1941

SHATTERING NEWS!! MY WORLD HAS FALLEN APART! Elisabet has been arrested by the Gestapo! Georg Dobring came to the embassy while I was having lunch with the Mosbys. He told us that the Foreign Ministry has received word that Elisabet has been taken into custody by the Gestapo at the Swiss border, on a charge of high treason. Somehow, Georg had known of my close relationship and said he would try to verify the information from friends working at Gestapo Headquarters on Prinz Albrecht Street.

My heart sank. Mosby tried to boost my spirits. The word was not official, he said, as if the Gestapo ever released official statements. We spoke to Kirstin. She promised to inquire further.

Later, Kirstin came into my office and told me "Elisabet is dead! She died after interrogation." She was executed without a trial on the basis of secret documents found in her possession.

'Sabette is dead! My dearest is dead! Elisabet is dead!

December 6, 1941

Kirstin informed me that it was unwise for the family to inquire about the body. If the SD so chose, they could release the remains or dispose 6of them in any way they desire. So, we do not even have her body to grieve over.

December 7, 1941

We were seated at the dinner table when the local block officer came to the door and whispered to Bruno Geulen. Bruno took a deep breath and approached the table looking grave.

Japan has declared war on the United States! Before the news could be digested, the telephone rang, and I was summoned back to the embassy.

Bradford and Mosby were in the communication room listening to the incoming instructions from Washington. The rest of us were gathered around radios digesting the BBC news flashes from London. Every so often one of the communication people would hand us a further update from Washington.

Incredible as it sounds, Japan has bombed the US fleet anchorage at Pearl Harbor, Hawaii, and sunk the entire Pacific fleet (excluding a few aircraft carriers which were not in harbor).

What now? Surely Mosby will be summoned back to the States. What about me? Does anyone know I am here?

We listened throughout the night, each report more ominous than the previous. The West Coast in danger of invasion! Hawaii guards against internal sabotage! Helen summed it up: "Chickens running around with their heads cut off."

December 8, 1941

The lion again in standing position. When I leaned over the table to pick up the cigar band, Herr Wing Collar whispered, "Good luck!"

Back at the embassy we examined the message. "Germany will declare war on the United States on December 10th." Three days away!

Bradford called Helen into his apartment and told her to stoke the furnaces! Priority One: all critical communications, etc. to be destroyed immediately. Priority Two and Three: less critical material, according to classification, to follow. The embassy was well prepared; even the non-American employees know the drill!

Bradford wanted Mosby and me out of Berlin on the next plane! No buts! No argument! And no families! He shares Mosby's concerns for his family, but his obligation to his country comes first! A flight to Lisbon leaves at 11 pm tonight. Both of us must be on it! Get moving!

After the embassy shutdown, he told us, the staff will be interned for several months in a nice, comfortable hotel in the German countryside, awaiting repatriation. He assured Mosby that his family would be well cared for.

I hung around while Mosby packed a valise and said his hurried goodbyes to Jean and Clayton. Vincent drove us to my home, where I quickly crammed a uniform in my valise.

Caterine and Fred watched me pack. I explained to Caterine that she was to continue to draw on the account at Weisbart's for the home and for Fred. As I threw my arms around them, the horn sounded. Fred was in tears.

The Geulens and Albrecht were standing at the curb. Words were needless. I squeezed their calloused hands and climbed in the car.

The Nazi officialdom gave us remarkably little trouble at Tempelhof Airport. Tomorrow will be a different story, when word gets out that our embassy is shutting down. As our Fokker Tri-motor circled over Berlin, I caught my last glimpse of that peculiar city, where I was leaving so much behind.

TANK COMMANDER

December 9, 1941

Morning found us checking into a small hotel in Lisbon. We handed in our passports at the front desk and then, while Dwaine went off to arrange transportation to the States, I settled into a lobby sofa and rested, while the chamber lady finished making up our rooms. I had developed a stiff neck and headache, which I attributed to the uncomfortable airplane ride; and resolved to spend the day in bed. While I rested, the clerk finished copying the required information from the passports and handed them back to me. I thumbed through the pages of Dwaine's passport and was astonished to learn that his family name was Harmon, not Mosby, and that he was six years older than the age he gave me. The deception was troubling, but I tried not to dwell on it, especially with a raging headache. I showered quickly and lay down to sleep.

December 18, 1941

I awoke in bed in a strange room devoid of furniture and saw an attractive Army nurse bending over me. To my astonishment, she told me that I was in Lajes Field, a US base in the

Azores, 800 miles off the coast of Portugal. I was their first patient. They weren't supposed to open until a week later, but there I was.

A young physician in white coat with lieutenant's bars on his shirt collar told me I had had a bout of aseptic meningitis. Virus, not bacteria, as they discovered after the spinal tap. He went on to explain that the illness is usually self-limiting and usually without unpleasant sequels. I should be ready to leave in a few more days.

Also, he handed me a brief note from a General Harmon. It said that he was compelled to leave before me, but was assured that I would recover promptly. On my arrival at Washington, I was without fail to telephone him at the indicated number. Later that day, I got up from bed. My legs were wobbly, but my strength seemed to be returning.

December 22, 1941

The flight from Lajes Field was an unpleasant one. There were no passenger seats, so I sat on the floor of the C-47 airplane and felt the vibrations travel up and down my body. When we finally landed in Anacostia, a small military airfield across the river from Washington, I telephoned the number given me and asked the switchboard operator to get me General Harmon. It took ten minutes to find him. He seemed glad to hear my voice and promised to pick me up in twenty minutes.

A half hour later a big, black Cadillac pulled up to the entrance of the terminal, and Dwaine motioned me in. I was reassuring him of my health when he interrupted to tell me that he had to attend a small cocktail party, and invited me to come with him. After, he had something important to ask me.

The limousine entered a large estate past steel gates guarded by soldiers, who saluted as we drove by. It drew up to a side entrance, and the driver rushed out to open Dwaine's door.

A tall, thin man in his fifties was waiting on the steps. He tossed his cigarette on the ground and crushed it in a twisting motion with the sole of his shoe. The old man was waiting for him, he told Dwaine. A numb feeling came over me as I slowly began to realize where we were.

As we hurried along the corridors, Dwaine introduced me to his companion, a Mr. Harry Hopkins. I heard Hopkins say that the old man was terribly put out when Dwaine's father died. He was there at Hyde Park for the funeral, and of course, gave the eulogy. He called Dwaine's father, "the greatest influence in his life," and at the grave, asked to left alone with the casket. Hopkins was afraid his wheelchair might roll into the grave. When they came to fetch him, his face was covered with tears. First time Hopkins had ever seen him cry.

Dwaine did not reply. I hadn't shaved or showered and was dressed in rumpled pants and sweatshirt. I felt like a slob.

We came to a guard standing at a door, who told Wayne that the President was waiting for him.

Inside, a half dozen people were scattered around the room. In between the standing figures, I saw a man in a wheel chair. The President! I almost wet my pants. In a booming voice, he instructed Dwaine to take a head count. "Seven," Dwaine told him and left me out.

The seated figure poured seven neat measures of a liquid into a large shaker, followed by two extras "for good luck," as he called it. He then added the Vermouth and a "pinch of this and a dash of that," and to begin stirring vigorously. Finally, the contents were poured into seven glasses and each of the spectators reached for theirs. He invited suggestion for the toast. Someone suggested "victory," but the President said they had drunk to that yesterday. Instead, he proposed a toast to Dwaine, who had given seven years to the service of his country.

He asked Dwaine for a progress report on Eugenia and his godson. Dwaine told him they were still interned at the Grand Hotel in Bad Nauheim; but will be coming home in a few months, after the Swedish Red Cross charters a ship to take them back.

The President suggested that when they come, they stay with him at the White House until Dwaine can find a house for them. Dwaine thanked the president, but reported that he has already found a place in Maryland in the Catoctin Mountains, near the OSS base, where he will be stationed.

The president set his empty glass back on the table and reminded Dwaine that he was expected for dinner at seven. With that, he declared the meeting adjourned, and Hopkins wheeled him out through a side door.

As we walked along the corridors, Dwaine got to the point quickly. He was now the deputy head of the Office of Strategic Services in charge of operations and needed a first-class assistant. Would I like the job? He promised me all the excitement I could hope for.

No, I told him. I'm an Army officer. I lead men in battle.

He was sorry to hear that. If there were anything he could do for me, I have only to telephone the White House. They'll know where to find him. And with that, he bade me a Merry Christmas and strode briskly down the corridor.

A taxi took me to the BOQ in Ft. Myers. On the way we passed the huge, newly completed office building. The traffic was exasperating. It took us a full hour before we reached out destination.

My old friend—now a sergeant—was sitting behind the desk, reading the sports page. On his desk were two children's books. When he saw me, he jumped up, overjoyed and let me know that his biggest thrill in life is when his grandchildren ask him to read them a fairy tale.

December 23, 1941

The Military Office Building, which everyone calls the "Pentagon," was teaming with humanity. I waited on line ten minutes for the civilian at the information desk to tell me how to reach the Office of the Chief of Staff (OCS).

The corridors swarmed with traffic moving in both directions. Some young soldiers moved briskly on roller skates with rubber wheels. It took twenty minutes before I found the office of the COS, which now filled an entire wing.

I gave my name to a sergeant seated behind a typewriter and asked to see General Brooks Moore, Deputy Chief of War Plans. The Sergeant consulted a list and informed me that General Moore was no longer here and that the Deputy Chief is now a full Chief of War Plans.

The Adjutant, Major O'Connor, was away from his desk but would be back in a few minutes.

Twenty minutes later, a studious Major O'Connor appeared, barely concealing his fatigue. He led me into the office of the Chief of War Plans, General Dwight Eisenhower, a husky blue-eyed officer with thinning hair and a broad smile.

Major O'Connor explained to the general that his predecessor had sent me to Berlin as military attaché. I was the one who had furnished the dates for all the Nazi invasions. Eisenhower remarked that it was a nifty piece of work. O'Connor also mentioned that I had been sending in observations about the German tank operations. Some of my reports had been passed around.

Eisenhower replied that he had seen my reports and supposed that I now wanted an assignment. He thought a while, then stood up and went to look at the wall map of military installations. After studying it, he returned to his seat and explained the situation:

Four armored divisions are now being formed, each with a tank brigade and two mobile infantry brigades. Each tank brigade has 1–2 tank regiments and a regiment of mobile infantry. Now suppose a small combat tank force is needed to meet an emergency. Until now, a brigade would have to be broken up to provide the necessary manpower. But General Marshall, our Chief of Staff, believes there is a place for an independent tank regiment which can be rapidly deployed, without having to break apart a brigade and leave some men standing idle.

And that's what General Marshall wants: an independent tank regiment.

Because of the present demands, General Eisenhower cannot hope to set me up for at least four weeks. By then, our barracks should be completed. I was told to plan to begin a month from now in North Carolina. I will be getting tank personnel previously trained at Fort Knox. Unfortunately, they have been trained in M-2's and M'3 tanks, so they will have to be retrained once the M-4's (Shermans) arrive.

My rank will be Lt Colonel, (temporary, of course). From Captain (temporary) to Lt. Colonel (temporary) in one jump. Hot dog!

After listening to the usual cautions, I saluted and followed Major O'Connor out the door.

The next hour I spent with O'Connor and staff while they cut my orders and notified the district command, before finishing up with me. At the PX, I bought my silver oak leaves and the other insignias and placed an order for another uniform. The sergeant at the BOQ wanted to move me into the senior BOQ, but I asked to remain where I was for the night.

January 28, 1942

For the past week, I have been at Fort Knox, Kentucky, attending a course on the new M-4 tank (which the British call the Sherman) and have been hard at work studying its manual. These are the 'specs on the M-4:

Air-cooled, aircraft, radial engine delivering 400 horsepower at 2.400 rpm. Two gas tanks holding 175 gallons of high test aviation gas, giving it a range of 120 miles. Overhaul after every 2,500 miles. On the sloped glacis in front, 2 ½ inches of armor. An auxiliary generator to provide extra power and warm the crew in cold weather.

Five men crew standing on two levels: upper level, the gunner (left), the loader-radio man (right), and the tank commander (back). Lower level, the driver (left), and the relief driver (right). Five shift gears, overdrive and one reverse. Steering done by balancing the two brakes.

Four entry/exit hatches; 5 periscopes with 360-degree traverse; 2 slots for direct vision, covered by bulletproof glass (not all tanks have this.) Frequency modulated radio, the 3CR 508, generating 30 watts with 10 pre-sets (stations).

Short barrel 75mm gun with a muzzle velocity of 2,300 fps, capable of penetrating 3 inches of straight steel but only at point blank range (!). In addition, 3 machine guns: .50 caliber (tank commander); one .30 caliber coupled to the 75mm gun, (gunner) and the 30 caliber (relief driver).

Formidable, at least on paper. Certainly a match for the Pz-IV. I hope.

February 15, 1942

For the first time since arriving at Camp Arnold, I assembled all my officers for a conference. Talk of wooden barracks had proved to be illusory. We had spent a grueling month setting up the pyramidal tents, mess halls and the schools (driving, gunnery and radio communication, motor and tank repair, first aid, etc.). Fortunately, we got our instructors from within our own military district, so transferring them to the 324 Combat Tank Regiment was easier than if they came from outside the district, and we were compelled to go through Washington.

I quickly reviewed our table of organization: 5 tanks to a platoon, 3 platoons to a company, 3 companies to a battalion and 3 battalions to the regiment, etc., etc., etc.

There were three things to remember: First, each tank must use its best driver, best gunner and best radio man, but each tanker must be able to perform every other job in the tank, so that in the event of shell damage, the tank might still function.

Second. The tanker must also be a good soldier: know how to care for his body, his uniform, his tank. He must know how to salute and how to shoot. In order for him to give his best effort, he must be in good physical health. That means proper attention to dental needs, bowels, tonsils, hernias and pilonidal cysts. The time to handle these things is now, not when we are in the field.

Three. The tanker must be able to march 20 miles to save his life. If his tank were to be hit, he must be able to make it back to his own line or surrender and risk being shot. So, we'll march—soldiers and officers alike, including the commanding officer, the doctor and the chaplain.

Training schedules have been drawn up. Every officer will be given a copy. The M-4 Sherman tanks are beginning to arrive. Let's get going.

March 27, 1942

The training has progressed faster than I could
have hoped for. The men were delighted with
the new M-4. There are seats for everyone and
even a small fan for summer and a duct for
engine heat in the winter. We found that by
having one company compete with the other,
the soldier puts extra effort into the drill. At the
gunnery range we found that because a man
excelled on the 75mm canon, he wasn't
necessarily expert with the .30 or .50 machine
gun. Truck drivers had an inside track for the
tank driver's job; civilian hunters for the
gunner; radio vacuum tube builders for radio
operator and repairmen; but it didn't always
work that way.

Unfortunately, we could not get the M I carbine
and had to settle for the .45 Colt 1911 pistol.

The march was another thing. As expected, the
headquarters staff squawked, but when they
saw the whole regiment lined up on the road,
including the officers, they became more
compliant. Five weeks have passed, and we
have reached our goal of 10 miles (and 10

return). In short, we are becoming a competent outfit.

May 14, 1942

Our first exercise. We're part of the White Army, composed of the 2nd Armored Division, the 324th Combat Tank Regiment, and others

We arrived at the Welkat area, South Carolina, after a 5-day march, and were handed a packet of papers, dealing with rules, tactics, organization; and containing a few deplorable maps of the area.

I read through the material carefully. It was vague and in some sections, contradictory. So far as the 324 Tanks were concerned, we had been given a hopeless assignment. In front of us, we have an impassable tank terrain, like a quagmire. When the exercise commences, we are ordered to advance. The only way to do so was by two state roads flanking the quagmire; but if we take those roads, we will certainly be stopped by the pre-fixed artillery and anti-tank guns of the Red Army. Net result—stopped cold, and all our trouble getting here will have been wasted.

I heard S/Sgt Carrol give permission for a corporal to buy some Coke Cola at a nearby Esso gas station, and I asked the corporal to bring us back a road map of South Carolina. The corporal returned in a half hour and handed me the map, which I studied carefully. The roads were well laid out, and I located the maneuver grounds and a few of its natural features. We were here at Steuben, and the enemy headquarters is here at Albion, twelve miles away on the other side of the quagmire.

I studied the map carefully. Was there a thin black line running through the quagmire all the way to Albion? I studied it for a few minutes, then asked S/Sergeant Carrol to look. He adjusted the lamp and studied the map, holding it up to his eyes. He reported that he, too, saw a small, unimproved road going through the quagmire to Albion.

I called to my executive officer, Major Ted Crosby, and told him to take a jeep down this road and see if it will support an M-4 Sherman; but not to let himself be seen. He came back in a hour and reported that M-4 tanks could get through in daylight and dry weather.

Just what I wanted. We notified Platoon 1, Company A, to be ready to proceed at 6 am tomorrow to the Red Army headquarters at Albion and to keep circling the command tent until I arrive.

May 15, 1942

I hardly slept last night. At 0600 the tanks started to roll along the unimproved road. Fortunately, the weather had been dry all this week. They arrived at Albion and identified the command tent by two stars flying from a pennant above the tent.

They started to circle the tent, and I cut in and followed them around. Several times an enraged occupant of the tent rushed out in pajamas to yell at the tankers. Finally, a yellow jeep drove up with an "umpire" sign hanging from the rear. The officer held up his hand, and I stopped the procession.

Infuriated, he said that I had used an unauthorized map and must stop this nonsense. He asked for my name and command, and ordered me to return at once to my starting point in Steuben.

I led the tanks back to Steuben, and spent the next hour looking to see if the instructions prohibit the use of unauthorized maps. They do not. When the umpire discovers that, he will not report me. Bet on it!

May 16, 1942

Our orders call for the 324 Tank Regiment to move down the two flanking roads. As expected, the enemy "destroyed" us with artillery and antitank guns. We were knocked out, but no unfavorable comment was made against us. The personnel reports were mediocre, but someone had written "highly innovative" in a space beside my name.

October 22, 1942

"Operation Torch." Order received to prepare for embarkation from Hampton Roads, Virginia. Destination unknown. The tankers have been given the new combat boots Patton had ordered for us and also the carbine rifles to replace the Colt .45s. A pool (about which I am supposed to know nothing) has been started in the 324, and the man who first correctly guesses our destination wins the total, minus

10% for the organizer. Officers disqualified from entering.

The 324 Combat Tank Regiment has successfully completed its preliminary training, if an outfit can ever be said to have done that. Morale is good, especially after the South Carolina maneuvers. The umpires gave us only a fair rating, but we earned a barrel of laughs, as word spread about a general running around in pajamas.

October 28, 1942

The march to Hampton Roads was vexing. Some of it was by train, which had its own share of difficulties. We arrived today at Hampton Roads. I had sent an advance party to scout the area.

A surprise awaited us. Part of the regiment was ordered to board a C-2 cargo ship; the remainder, a long vessel, which they call a LST (Landing Ship Tank). In fact, ours was the first LST ever built (?), and it was still considered experimental. The ship has two decks, the upper one for our half-tracks, jeeps and trucks;

the lower for 24 tanks. The rest of the regiment would be loaded onto a regular C-2 freighter.

I was ordered to take notes on the LST performance. Its front ramp was lowered, and our lighter vehicles moved directly in the ship and were lifted up, by elevator, to the upper deck. Then the tanks rolled in. Loading on the LST went quickly, while hours later on the freighter, the cranes were still bringing the vehicles aboard.

The LST is a clumsy, gangling giant, which is the price one pays for the convenience. The tankers were berthed between decks, and early suffered from *mal de mer* ("Molly Meyer"). Even so, the trip has been uneventful (thank God), considering that many of my men had never been to sea before, and some have never even seen the sea. We travel at 10 knots and seem to be part of a huge operation that has the name "Operation Torch." No doubt the people on the freighters have been given complete information, but we on the LST are in the dark. Where are we headed for? Dakar? France? Suez?

The LST captain tells me that the overall commander of Torch is General George Patton, who is known to be a strict disciplinarian. His Chief of Staff is a General Hobart Gay, and the ADC is a Colonel Charles Codman, an ex-Bostonian wine dealer. Our captain says that this is the largest amphibious operation ever, which I can believe since I have already counted over 100 ships.

November 8, 1942

We're here! We arrived at Fedella, a small roadstead about 8 miles north of Casablanca, Morocco, (familiar to movie-goers). The LST drew up to the shore, let down its ramp, the tank engines started up and off they went. The other ships were not so lucky. There were periodic 14-inch salvos fired by a French battleship, the Jean Bart, which is docked in the harbor at Casablanca. This is information told me by the officers who have come ashore from the other ships. A French light cruiser and other French ships were also firing at us. Had they struck the transports, we would have had thousands of casualties.

Since there is no pier, the transports are off-loading vehicles by cranes onto landing rafts and small landing transports, which bob up and down in the deep swell, often with loss of life and vehicles. Despite the heavy swell and the enemy firings, the landings were proceeding in a semi-orderly fashion.

I arrived with the first of my tanks and led them to a large empty area a half mile from the harbor. There they began to set up camp, while still maintaining vigilance. I went down to the roadstead to meet the incoming tanks and vehicles arriving by landing boats from the freighters. They were slow in appearing, hours after the tanks in the LST had landed.

The beach was in a state of indescribable confusion. Soldiers swarmed over the beach looking for their units. Jeeps were parked helter-skelter, their drivers uncertain where to go and what to do. Small groups of French soldiers wandered along the shore, wondering what was going on. No one paid them any attention. Bodies of luckless soldiers lined the water's edge, whose landing craft had overturned or who had been struck by rounds fired from the French warships. Africa or not, the water was frigid.

I saw a clump of what appeared to be corpses near the water's edge, but one of the corpses scratched his nose. When I asked what was going on, a corporal told me that a nest of enemy snipers were firing at them from the building in front, and their M-1 Garand rifles were waterlogged.

I walked to the nearby brick building and in French asked the men inside what they were doing. A drunken voice replied that they were repelling foreign invaders.

Foreign invaders! They are Americans! I ordered them to come out and motioned the soldiers to stand up out of the water.

A few minutes later the three French soldiers emerged from the building to stare at us. After a good look at the soaked invaders, they walked away in the direction of Casablanca.

Standing in his jeep, the beachmaster control officer relayed by radio the location of my regiment to the Augusta, Patton's command ship. The order came back for the 324 Tank Regiment to send out a reconnoitering detail.

I searched my jeep for a pair of flags— American and French—which I had bought in a flag store in Hampton Roads before embarkation; and had my driver mount them on each side of the vehicle. The stupid little episode with the three French soldiers convinced me that the French do not want to fight us. We have only to show them a way to stop without besmirching their honor.

We started up the road to Casablanca in my jeep. About two miles from the landing zone we came to a lone French soldier standing guard at the road, with his bicycle lying on the ground. I signaled the driver to stop and asked in French for the name of his officer. The Frenchman told us the officer was stationed in an encampment 3 miles down the road. We arrived at a small camp with a dozen tents pitched beside the road. A sentry challenged us and when the captain appeared, I asked that he take me to the commanding officer of the Casablanca military garrison. He replied that without orders, he couldn't help me. I told him to unbuckle his holster and take out his pistol. He has just captured an enemy officer and is taking him to the Commandant for questioning.

The magic formula. He immediately understood and climbed into the front seat. On we rode past a dozen large encampments into the city. Casablanca looked like what I imagined it to be, a French provincial city, with Cinzano awnings, sidewalk cafes and a sprinkling of Arabic signs. People in European and some native dress huddled nervously at street corners.

An idea came to me as we rode through the city. I asked my captor where the big brass eat. "At Marcel's," he told me. Three blocks from the command building, he pointed to a well maintained French restaurant with an awning and a handsome polished brass entrance.

We entered, and I asked to see the proprietor. Marcel himself came out, reluctantly, from the kitchen, a small, haughty man with a pencil mustache and a distrustful attitude. He was angry that I dared come without an appointment. That bothered me. I let him know in unrefined French that If he does not accommodate us, we'll burn down his restaurant and him with it. And the French officer assured him that I would do it.

I explained that I wanted to arrange a dinner tomorrow at 8 pm for ten high-ranking officers. Best food and his best wines and liquors. The drinks to be served beginning at 7 pm when the diners walk in. Also, a side table for the junior officers. Marcel was instructed to keep a careful account of the prices of the wines, cognac and champagnes and to bear in mind that the accounts will all be carefully scrutinized by the General's aide, Colonel Charles Codman, a professional wine dealer with the utmost perspicacity. Colonel Codman himself will settle the bill.

He agreed to do a good job, and I insisted that he do a memorable job.

Back in the jeep, I got the name of the French chief of staff, a General Albert Sevres. We drove to the nearby office building of the commandant, a drab, stone structure with two sentries and a corporal posted outside.

I asked to be taken to the chief of staff, General Sevres, a flabby middle-aged man with bushy eyebrows. The word "surrender" was never mentioned. I explained to him that General George Patton, our commanding officer, wished to invite General Charles Nogues, the commandant, and four of his senior staff to a dinner tomorrow at 7 pm at Marcel's. General Patton hopes that their number will include some of the splendid French officers who served with him in the Saint Mihiel sector in the last war. "That will be me!" General Sevres exclaimed, already warming to the idea.

After arranging the details, we exchanged salutes and I left, dropping off the captain along the way. By the time we got back to the beach, the cannon fire had quieted down. Someone said that the Jacque Bart had been sunk by planes from an American aircraft carrier. Since the details of the forthcoming dinner could not be settled over the radio, I went by boat to the Augusta and asked to see the Chief of Staff General Hobart Gay or Patton's aide, a Colonel Charles Codman, the former wine dealer, who is well-liked in the command.

When I explained the arrangements, General Gay was skeptical, but Colonel Codman was immediately enthusiastic and promised to examine thoroughly the charges for the dinner.

[General George Patton met General Charles Nogues November 9, 1942. An agreement was reached, and on the following day the fighting ceased. Until his departure, General Patton was the figurative commandant of Casablanca, but the actual governing was performed by General Nogues.]

December 12, 1942

The 324th is encamped two miles outside the city. Life has become very tame and uninteresting. General Patton rides around the city in a black limousine, heralded by the shrieking sirens of his motorcycle escort. The 2nd Armored Brigade and most of the mobile infantry have long since left for Oran, in preparation for the Allied drive into Tunisia, while the 324 Combat Tank Regiment in Casablanca drills, swims, plays baseball and keeps out of trouble. I am quite astonished to see how well behaved the men are. The chaplain has a long list of poor townspeople who need help with carpentry and plumbing, and he never wants for volunteers. In what other Army would you find men like these?

We are told that General Marshall still fears an invasion by the Spanish from Spanish Morocco, and wants the 324 Tank Regiment to be ready to engage them.

December 17, 1942

Our men have long ago given up looking for Rick's *Café Americaine* (although four bars have since laid claim to the honor). Soldiers stroll the streets, carefully monitored by vigilant MP's. Since almost all of the soldiers come to the bordellos just to look, we have made an arrangement with the madames to sell the soldier a glass of red wine for $2, so the house can make a profit. Dozens of Berber kids hang around our encampment, just to watch the baseball games. Judging from all the candy given them, I'm afraid they'll have tooth problems the rest of their lives.

(Bizerte and Tunis are on the Mediterranean coast of Tunisia, both held, by the German army of General von Arnim, and where the Germans land their supplies. South of the cities is a mountain range running north to south, traversed by several passes, held by the Americans, under the command of General Lloyd Fredendall. Rommel's army is approaching from Libya to the east, pursued by General George Montgomery.

Rommel's plan is to reach the south of Tunisia and establish a defense at the Mareth Line, a 40-mile defense strip between the east side of the mountains and the sea. Since he wants to prevent American troops in the west of Tunisia from moving through the passes to threaten his flank; he has sent troops to both passes, and on. February 19, 1942 his troops defeated the American army at El Guetlar and Kasserine, sending them reeling back to the west. [Great confusion in the American lines.)

February 21, 1943

We have received word that General Patton has being ordered to take command of the American II Corps, formerly commanded by General Lloyd Fredendal (and has been promoted to Lt. General). One might think that the 324th Combat Tank Regiment would also be also summoned, but here we sit, preparing for a mythical invasion from Spanish Morocco.

The departure of General Patton compels the Casablanca Government to release from its prison the Gaullists, newspaper editors and the Jews whom the Nogues government has kept imprisoned, with the tacit consent of Washington and General Patton, as the price for maintaining peace with the Vichy French supporters. There is celebration in the streets, since most of the French now support de Gaulle and the Free French.

February 26, 1943

An order has been received (finally) for the 324 Combat Tank Regiment to leave Casablanca and proceed to Bougie, Algeria on the Mediterranean coast and from there to report to General Patton at Tebesse, Algeria 125 miles inland.

No mention of how to get there. Someone suggested an overland march across Morocco and Algeria. When I discussed this with the French army officers (Vichy), they scoffed at the idea and told me that marching a mobile regiment across 400 miles of desert can't be done! Rommel and Montgomery's march was different. They went along the sea. Other French officers (De Gaulle) told me that General Leclerc is doing that very thing at this very moment: marching from Lake Chad to the sea. Two opinions. Take your choice. Later, I found that we could have gone by train, since there was an uncertain rail connection between Morocco and Algeria that would have accommodated one tank per rail car. There was no assurance, however, that it would arrive before the end of the century.

March 1, 1943

To be on the safe side, I called for sea transport to take us to Algeria, hoping they would send LST's. Our luck ran out. They sent 2 freighters, which arrived this morning.

March 4, 1943

We have a two-destroyer escort. It's been a long and boring trip. The air blowers below decks broke down; the food is tasteless, and the crew unfriendly.

March 6, 1943

We arrived at Bougie, Algeria, and proceeded to off-load at a pier. This greatly speeded up the unloading. After assembling our unit, we set out for Tebesse, Algeria, 125 miles inland, the staging place for the II Corps (Patton).

March 11, 1943

Reached Patton's headquarters in Tebesse, and reported in to General Gay, the chief of staff. He told me that he did not need us, but—and here he picked up a dispatch to refresh his memory—there's a place for us at Mareth with General Bernard Montgomery of the British Army.

Monty had finally arrived in Tunisia, only to be confronted by the Mareth Line, held by Rommel's men. As is his custom, Montgomery immediately requested reinforcements, which Patton was reluctant to provide, until the 324 Combat Tank Regiment showed up, and he found the perfect solution. We were told to report to General Montgomery.

March 22, 1943

We made our way with great difficulty through the Central Mountain Range now in American hands, and came up from the south to where General Montgomery and the British 8th Army were dug in, facing the Mareth Line.

Montgomery was a small, nervous fellow, with tired eyes and a bushy mustache. He was displeased to learn that we were his only reinforcements—a combat tank regiment. I saluted smartly and told him what an honor it was to serve under a real soldier. (After all, he had 5 years in the trenches of WW I; Eisenhower had none; Patton had 4 days). His attitude immediately changed, and he instructed his Adjutant to see that we were given everything we needed. We were ordered to take a position on the far left (west) of the line and to guard against a flank attack.

While we waited at British Army HQ for water and fuel, British tank commanders poured in, telling of combat with the new Pz V, the "Panther," which had recently been landed in Bizerte and found their way here. Until now, I had not heard of the Panther, but the reports stirred my interest.

Each report sounded more alarming than the one before. They also spoke of (but had not seen) another new monster, the Pz 6 known as the Tiger, supposed to have an 88 gun, if you can believe it! No wonder the British were disturbed. Before the arrival of the Panther, the British thought they (and the U.S.) were king of the mountain with the Sherman M-4. I suppose it was inevitable that the Germans would seek a tank to match the Soviet T-34, which had surprised them in the 1941-2 winter battle outside Moscow, but I did not realize they would get them so soon.

March 23, 1943

We took our position at the far end of the British line and, upon orders, began to fire at the enemy. The Mareth Line consisted of dense pillboxes, forts and battlements which the French had constructed in 1940 to withstand the threatened invasion of the Italians from Libya, but the structures were not first-class and some of the pillboxes had begun to crumble.

March 25, 1943

We have now spent two days firing at the enemy position. The British command has been very attentive to our needs and kept us well supplied with water and provisions.

So far, no sign of German tanks in my sector. I decided to force the issue and sent for my artillery officer, Captain Ed Wyman. He had stationed our two tank destroyers in the mountain overlooking our sector of the Mareth Line.

When Wyman came, I pointed to a dip in the ground ahead of us, large enough to house two tanks and ordered him to pre-fix his guns on the area in front of the hollow, then move his guns out of sight of the enemy. When the enemy tanks reached the hollow, he was to reposition his anti-tank guns and knock out the first German tank (hopefully a Panther) with a 105 armor-piercing round from his howitzer, and the second (Panther?) with a phosphate round from our 75mm tank destroyer.

He protested that the phosphate would not stop the tank, and actually, he was right. The phosphate round will not pierce the armor, but it will cause a fire on the surface and send smoke into the tank. The rule in the German tank corps—which I remember from my Berlin days—was that a tank crew cannot abandon their tank unless it is on fire. So, I was hoping that the phosphate round would deceive them into leaving the tank.

March 26, 1943

Morning, I sent two M-4 Sherman's into the dip and told them to commence firing at the enemy line. Sure enough, a half-hour later two large enemy tanks (Panthers!!) emerged from the German line and moved toward the hollow to open fire. Following orders, our tanks quickly began their retreat. As the Panthers began to fire, our two anti-tank guns on the mountain slope opened up. The 105 Howitzer hit the first Panther and destroyed it with a big AP round, while the anti-tank 75 performed perfectly with a phosphate round to the glacis (front) of the other Panther, and left it smoking badly. Two minutes later, the hatch flew open and the German tankers began racing back to their line.

The tank continued to smoke, so that it could not be entered. I wanted that tank badly, but if I left it there, the Germans might send out a repair tank and snatch it from us. Toward evening, I went back with our rescue and repair vehicle and tried covering the side of the tank with foam. It seemed to work, so that by wearing an oxygen mask I could climb in to look around. On the shelf next to a shell storage area, I saw a Pz V tank manual. Hot dog! Quickly I exited the tank with manual in hand, and we drove back.

March 27, 1943

I spent that night studying the manual until I knew the contents well enough, then before daybreak we drove back, and I got the tank moving toward our lines. I could see immediately that the Panther had a better turning radius and better sighting optics than the M-4. A mighty cheer greeted us on my return, and the men quickly named the beast "the Manning Panther." We spent the day testing the Panther, and I allowed some of my best drivers to work the controls. The men with cameras took dozens of photographs.

March 28, 1943

The siege is winding down. British intelligence officers report that the enemy is withdrawing from the Mareth Line and joining up with General Arnim in the north. The British command sent for me, I was told that General Montgomery had no further need for the 243 Tank Regiment and that we were to report back to General Patton.

April 2, 1943

We left our position and travelled back, this time through the pass, to General Patton's command, with the "Manning Panther "leading the parade. Once there, they insisted that we paint a white star on the turret of the Panther, so that it would not be mistaken for a German vehicle. Also, that we turn the turret whenever we pass through a settlement. so that the village people can see the star.

General Patton merely acknowledged us with a grunt. General Gay told us that our services were no longer required and that we were to return to Casablanca to resume protecting

Morocco from a Spanish invasion. But they kept the Manning Panther.

[May 13, 1943

The Axis forces in North Africa surrender. Approximately 275,000 German and Italian prisoners taken]

May 15, 1943

We had a long stay in Bougie, Algeria, awaiting transportation. Most of the shipping is being readied to take the Allied armies to their next destination (some say Sicily); and the enemy POWs to prison camps in the US). Our turn finally came. Two run-down APA troop transports.

May 22, 1943

The trip took nearly a week, and we were almost overjoyed to be back in Casablanca. The white houses in the hills seemed to glisten, and the kids on the docks seemed happy to see us again.

August 16, 1943

We've been back for five weeks and everyone is bored. The news reports say that our troops are doing well in Sicily and have almost driven the four German divisions from the island.

Today we received word that a Congressman will be arriving to inspect the 324th Combat Tank Regiment. We've been inspected before by Congressmen, but never by one who is making a special trip to look us over. Does that mean he has a nephew serving in the 324? Anyway, the visit will put us on our toes. Woe to the officer whose men slip up!

August 18, 1943

The congressman landed at the Port Lyaute airport and motored down to us. His name is Congressman Alfred McWirther from Nebraska—fifth term in Congress and vice-chairman of the Armed Services Committee. A pleasant, soft spoken man with shrewd eyes and a no-nonsense manner.

He reviewed the regiment without comment. Instead of the grand tour of Casablanca, he wanted to speak with me in private. I took him into my tent and had another chair brought in. He said that he was here because his fellow congressmen have been shown tons of letters written from soldier to parent about a new German tank which has been devastating our own M-4 Shermans.

He lit up a cigarette and continued. His fellow Congressmen sent him to find out what's going on. When he asked General Patton, he was told that the new German tank—the "Panther"—is no match for our own M-4 Sherman. Except that when the congressman asked around, the soldiers told him differently. He had also learned that I had captured a Panther and had examined it. So that makes me one of the few who knows what he is talking about. What about it? Is this tank as good as everyone says it is?

I hesitated, but only for a moment. An Army officer is expected to go through channels when communicating with a Congressman, On the other hand, what is this country coming to when a U.S. Congressman cannot get an honest answer; and I was determined to give him one.

I told him that the Pz V Panther is a good tank now, and will be even better when they iron out the trouble with its transmission and its tracks. It was put into production before it could be thoroughly tested in the factory, so they're testing it on the battlefield—the most demanding and authoritative kind of test. A few M-4's might be able to maneuver around the Panther and disable it with some hits to its flank or rear, but tank for tank the M-4 is at a great disadvantage.

My immediate concern is that we have been issued High Explosive ammunition, which does not easily penetrate the tank armor; instead of the armor-piercing shell, which can penetrate. This is a holdover from antiquated military thinking that the purpose of the tank was for infantry support, while tank defense was entrusted, not to the tanks themselves, but to the anti-tank destroyers. About optimum tank size, I can see the difficulties with a heavy tank. They are too big and too heavy to be transferred from ship to landing craft, so the only way they can be off-loaded, is to ensure that the ship is berthed at a pier. No pier, no heavy tank (unless they are carried by a LST, which so far are few,in number.)

He asked if we need a heavier tank, and I told him that we do, but that it may be too late to develop one now. However, we might be able to install a bigger 76mm gun on the M-4. Montgomery's officers told me the British working on a 7 mm, 17-pounder gun to go on a M-4 body ("the firefly").

The M-4 is a fine tank, I told him. It can travel huge distances without breaking down and is reasonably fast. It can be easily repaired, its parts are interchangeable, but it's just no match for the heavier armor and heavier 76.2 cannon on the Panther.

He thanked me for the information and asked what a fine outfit like the 324 Battle Tank Regiment was doing in Casablanca? I told him about the fear in Washington of an invasion from Spanish Morocco, and he snorted with laughter.

September 4, 1943

Weeks have gone by. At one time I had hoped the 324 would receive a commendation for capturing the Manning Panther, but nothing ever came of it. We parade on French holidays, visit the hospitals and the orphanage. The De Gaulle Free French have now taken over the government, and there is little evidence left of the Vichy administration.

(The Allied Armies landed on September 3, 1943 in southern Italy at Salerno, Calabria and Taranto and are driving north.)

September 10, 1943

The 324th has just finished a practice march to Port Lyautey and back. It went without a hitch, but the men cannot help from feeling blah.

September 14, 1943

Hooray! Orders from Washington. The 324 is to be withdrawn from Casablanca and transported to an unstated destination. Italy? Most say Italy, but we will soon find out.

September 18, 1943

The 324 has embarked on two transport ships, the SS. Warren and the SS. Worthington, and we're off to the unknown. We are now 3 days out, sailing without an escort. To relieve the monotony, I arranged for a different group of 10 men to tour the engine room twice daily, and another party to visit the bridge. The men from the bridge tour report that we are sailing due west. But to where?

September 26, 1943

We are now 10 days at sea. The ships now have a 4-vessel escort. The men from the bridge tour report that we are now sailing north northeast. They were told by the mate that the western course had been necessary to escape the danger of submarine attack, but now that we have the escort, we can resume our true course. To where?

October 1, 1943

We've landed at Larne, a quiet sea town in Northern Ireland! Our orders are to proceed to Strabane in the lush countryside to train for service in continental Europe. That implies a landing in France, doesn't it?

October 6, 1943

We are in Albry, 40 miles from nowhere in a beautiful countryside. The families are friendly, especially when our men volunteer their services on the nearby farms, which are desperately short of labor. Seldom are there infractions of the law. The two reports of attempted rape were so unbelievable that the police refused further investigation.

We have been given a strict training schedule. Now we fire the tank's 75's, rather than those of the field artillery. Same for the .30 and .50 machine guns. We are also obliged to pass the infantry obstacle course, including the 30-foot climb, the river rope crossing and the barbed wire crawl with live rounds firing overhead. The men are taught to dig fox holes instead of trenches, since the enemy tanks can roll over the depression, make a half turn and, in so doing, crush all the men in the trench.

October 10, 1943

I have met Fiona, a young Lincolnshire math student, who is teaching in a local school for the duration. We have become very good friends.

October 13, 1943

On the move again. This time to Warrenport, North Ireland, where we are embarking for Liverpool. There was barely time to send a hurried goodbye note to Fiona.

October 15, 1943

We docked, off-loaded and started off for Scarborough in northeastern England. Along the way, there were stops, where the Red Cross served tea, which some men drank for the first time. The towns we passed seemed pleasant to the eye, but our encampment is in a remote plain, off by itself.

October 17, 1943

We are back on our training schedule, but now we have close supervision by the 3rd Armored Brigade. Some say we are part of the III Army and our commanding officer is our old friend, George Patton, who has been kept in mothballs since slapping a GI in Sicily.

We drill from sunrise to sunset in all kinds of simulations and are given grades, like in school. One unit competes with another—regiment against regiment—so we're always on our toes.

October 26, 1943

Lately, we have begun to work conjointly with the 41st Mobile Infantry Regiment. Working with another unit seems strange, but we're getting used to it. Major Ted Crosby, my executive, seems to think we're being formed into a brigade. Our counterpart, the 84th Tank Regiment, has arrived and is camped 5 miles away. They are fresh from the States and as green as a shamrock.

November 15, 1943

A visit today from our distinguished commander, General George S. Patton. He arrived with the sound of sirens screaming from his motorcycle escort. He wears a tailored, special-order uniform with polished cavalry boots and he carries a riding crop. Shades of the 1880 raj!

Nothing was good enough for George. The best we got out of him was a grunt. When I was first introduced, and I told him my name, he thought for a moment, and then his aide whispered something in his ear. He looked at General Gay and then at me, but said nothing. When he saw my men emerging from their tanks wearing only a helmet liner instead of a helmet, all he did was to tell his adjutant to make a note of it. No fines. No reprimands. No comments.

March 4, 1944

Spring has come. Everyone is talking about the impending invasion of the Continent, but we have not been trained for amphibious landings. Nor have we been issued D Day landing kits. We just keep training. We're now the 5th Armored Brigade, but we are not yet attached to any division. Our shoulder patches have not changed. We still wear the 324 Tank Regiment tag.

June 8, 1944

D Day has come and gone; and the Fifth
Armored Brigade is still encamped in northeast
England, still drilling. Rumor is that we are
being prepared for a Norway invasion. Except,
wouldn't we be given amphibious training? We
are now officially in the III Army, under
Georgie Porgy.

July 16, 1944

Orders to proceed to Southhampton for
embarkation to France! Finally!. The D Day
landings have been going on for several weeks.
All that our troops have accomplished so far (it
seems to me), is a circumscribed lodgment in
the Normandy countryside. I daren't use the
word, but we're STUCK. The British are
STUCK at Caen in the North and General
Hodges' 1st Army s STUCK in the south near
St. Lo.

July 25, 1944

We are now in the southern pocket of the
lodgment near St. Lo, France. First Army
artillery fired a terrific barrage two nights ago,

followed by a 1,500-allied plane attack on the German position. Yesterday morning the 1st Army moved forward, smashing the German defense at St. Lo, thereby permitting the newly-arrived 3rd Army (us) to pour through the gap without much resistance (Operation Cobra). The only opposition the 324 encountered was a panzer company of 14 Pz-IV's and two Pz-V (Panther), which our air squadrons harassed, and the 324 Tank Regiment finished off. Most of the Panthers and Tigers remain in the north, opposing the British army.

August 5, 1944

After pouring through the gap, the 3rd Army fanned out: one corps for Normandy; one corps for Brittany; and two corps to make a large circle and move north. Or at least that's what we were told. The 5th Armored Brigade (including the 324th Regiment) has been ordered to remain behind at Mortain, the site of the gap, to prevent the enemy from closing it off. We are considered a reserve unit, awaiting assignment to a corps.

August 7, 1944

The German 7th Army of General von Kluge has been ordered to attack the break-out gap at Mortain, France, in an effort to pinch it off, and trap all four American corps that have gone through. The 5th Armored (including the 324th Tank Regiment) has orders to stop him.

August 13, 1944

We have just undergone 6 days of the worst battle imaginable. Dead bodies and burned- out vehicles everywhere. The woods are still on fire. Thanks to our marvelous air support by the XIX Tactical Airforce under OP Weyland and our superb artillery, we were able to defeat the enemy, and they seem to be withdrawing, after losing half their tanks. But not before knocking out dozens of our M-4 (75) tanks, which functioned poorly against the few Panthers we had come across. But the new Sherman M-4's (76mm) are arriving, as replacements. These have a 76mm gun with much longer barrel, faster barrel twists, and greater muzzle velocity (more than 2,800 feet/sec ???) than does the M-4 (75)'s. Also, it has add-on steel plates affixed to the front and over the gas and fluid-covered weapon storage shelves to decrease the fire hazard. Great, but we need them now!

August 15, 1944

Received the first of the long barrel 76mm tanks. From now on our replacements will be the long barrel 76's (2,800 feet per second). No more 75 short-barrel (2,200 fps). What this means is that the M-4(76) Sherman can penetrate the glacis (front) of the Panther at 400 yds (????), rather than have to fire point blank. Also, the armor of the M-4(76) is heavier and its tracks wider, to more easily dig itself out of deep mud. Of course, our fire would have greater penetration, if we were given adequate supplies of the new super armor piercing ammunition, instead of the presently issued HE (high explosive) crap.

August 17, 1944

Direction northwest. Ordered to race to Argentan, against little opposition along the way. If we take Argentan and close ranks with the British, who are moving south from Caen to Falaise, we can pinch off the German retreat, trapping 100,000 German soldiers. The 5th

Armored Brigade (including the 324 Tank Regiment) are now assigned to the XII Corps of General Manton Eddy. All I know about the XII Corps, is that their spearhead is the 37th Armored Regiment led by Lt. Colonel Creighton Abrams, whom I had known at the Academy and who seemed to me to have had no great leadership talent as a cadet.

August 19, 1944

We have been travelling fast and furious. Surprisingly enough, our supplies have kept up with us. The 5th Armored brigade arrived after the others, so we occupy the periphery of the Argentan sector. The battle is well underway. Air attacks on the enemy position continue all day long.

August 20, 1944

Tremendous air bombardment of German troops near the Falaise gap, unfortunately killing some of our own men, as well as tens of thousands of Germans. We are waiting for the British to close their part of the gap, to trap the rest of the 7th Army of General von Kluge. I have tried to speak to some of the German prisoners. Most were almost witless from the incessant bombing, and I could get little out of them. The roads are blocked by an unending line of utterly destroyed German vehicles.

August 21, 1944

Montgomery failed to close the gap and 40,000 Germans have escaped. What a disappointment! (note: Montgomery had to face the largest number and heaviest armed of the German defenders)

August 26, 1944

Direction west. Proceeding south of Paris, with the completely disorganized enemy on the run. Like most of the men, I'm sorry we could not stop to see the fair city, but as long as we can get our supplies, we're moving west. Make hay while the sun shines, Patton tells us. My tanks are behaving surprisingly well, with few major repairs required *en route*. Our fuel comes from England, under the channel through a pipe line to Normandy and from there to here by truck, the Red Ball Express, driven by black quartermaster soldiers, who drive day and night. Round trip 3 days. They have completely abandoned the ancient Quartermaster driving regulations from 1926 and composed their own, but this cannot continue indefinitely without fatigue breaking down the system. We desperately need a large port, but nothing is available, since all the captured ports have been badly damaged and must first be repaired.

November 1, 1944

After crossing the Somme, Aisne and Meuse Rivers, the 5th Armored Brigade (including the 324th Tank Regiment) has reached Lorraine. No thought whatsoever to visiting my mother's birthplace. The weather has been raining and cold and the roads muddy. We've been forced to slow down because our supplies have had difficulty reaching us.

November 2, 1944

Our supplies have abruptly stopped. No sooner did we cross the Moselle River, when we had to halt and take up a defensive position until our supplies start up again.

November 5, 1944

Our supplies have resumed. We're now in muddy Lorraine, with its weary peasants, small towns and boarded-up windows. Patton is insistent on capturing Metz, our first large city; but its solid stone fortifications are formidable and thirty inches thick in some parts. We have attacked the forts guarding the city and have been repulsed. His staff opposes a direct attack and, instead, advise him to starve the city into surrender. Fewer casualties.

November 11, 1944

So far, we have gotten nowhere with a direct attack. The fortifications are formidable, and the city skillfully defended. Patton is not the magician he thought he was. On our attack on Fort Driant, guarding the approach to Metz, the 5th armored has lost 15 tanks with no gain.

November 15, 1944

We have broken off the direct attack and are now surrounding the city.

November 18, 1944

Metz has fallen. We are in the city. I wanted to visit the St. Stephen cathedral and see the stained-glass windows, but we had to keep moving.

December 15, 1944

We have reached the Westwall (Siegfried Line) and are planning the assault. The weather has turned cold and the sky overcast. The first snow has fallen. "Peace by Christmas" seems an unfulfillable dream. Meanwhile our attack up and down the line has stalled, and the troops are making plans for winter. Up north, the 1st Army (Hodges) has been having a hot time in the Huertgen Forest area, which is a part of the Siegfried Line complex. They have already lost 29,000 men!! The infantry has begun to suffer from frostbite, less so the tankers.

December 16, 1944

THIRD ARMY ALERT!!! We are ordered to proceed north with all speed. According to brigade briefing, while we were bothering Metz, the Germans have been assembling

200,000 men and 800 tanks and have sent them through the Ardennes Forest against four American Divisions, resting peacefully in the sector. Result: DISASTER. Where did all those German troops come from?

December 17, 1944

The enemy divisions have already broken out of the bulge and are proceeding toward Antwerp in an attempt to detach the American and British armies. General Hodge (1st Army) and General Simpson (9th Army) have been superseded by General Montgomery, who has been put in charge of containment of the Germans from the north.

December 18, 1944

Patton and the Third army have been called on to relieve Bastogne 125 miles away, a small village in the middle of the enemy penetration, occupied by American troops, who are interdicting the German supply column; so that the rampaging German tanks cannot bring up their own supplies and must capture ours. For the III Army to turn north means turning around 100,000 troops, thousands of tons of food and supplies, tens of thousands of jeeps, tanks, trucks and guns. No small job, but I'll say this. If anyone in the US Army can do it, old Georgie can. And he is still going to insist that the men in his command wear ties!

December 21, 1944

Direction north! The whole III Army has caught the Bastogne fever, and we're rushing north to relieve the town. The weather is miserable. Snow everywhere, roads iced, so that despite their new cleats, our new tanks skid off the road when they try to speed up. I feel sorry for those GIs who have to travel without cover, exposed to the icy blasts. That means the infantry and those of us, (like me) who travel in jeeps. or half-tracks. And don't tell me to ride inside a tank. How much can a commander see or hear from the inside?

December 22, 1944

Direction north! They say that two of our 4 armored divisions have already made contact with the enemy around Bastogne, but the town is still surrounded by the Germans.

December 25, 1944

We finally approached within 20 miles of Bastogne. The snow is deep and that forces our tanks to stay on the roads, which are mined and well-covered by pre-set German artillery. Fortunately, our infantry have penetrated German defenses and beginning to capture their artillery. Patton has split his column along three roads approaching the town. Our 5th Tank Brigade is on the western road along with the 4th Armored Brigade (Lt. Col. Creighton Abrams), who is determined to be the first to enter Bastogne. Me, I'd be happy to be the Tenth.

December 26, 1944

Bastogne has been reached and the town relieved. As expected, Lt. Col. Creighton Abrams and his 4th Tank Brigade were the first to arrive. The weather has cleared, and our fighters are swooping down on the enemy tanks. The German advance has been halted, and now they are going to be mauled.

January 4, 1945

The Third Army has been ordered to squeeze the bulge at Hauffalize, 15 miles away, where we hope that the Ist and 7th American Armies in the north can meet us, thereby trapping the German soldiers contained therein.

January 7, 1945

The Eddy XII Corps (including the 5th Armored) has reached Hauffalize and closed off the gap, but most of the Germans have already fled on foot or are preparing to surrender. This has been a brutally cold winter, so that a retreat on foot will be a nightmare for the enemy. Their huge gamble has failed. This comes when you entrust your Army to a Private First Class.

January 10, 1945

Hitler is continuing to withdraw his troops from the bulge. Everywhere we look, we see abandoned or damaged German vehicles and tanks. If ever the US Army wants to study German heavy tanks, it will find a forest of them here. The 324 has held up nicely. Many of the retreating German soldiers are on foot, but they carry handheld armor piercing guns (*panzerfaust, panzerschreck*), so we must be vigilant. We've already lost 5 tanks to those weapons.

Most of the replacement tanks are the M-4 (76), with the heavier gun (2,800 fps), water-encased ammunition racks and appliqué (welded on) armor over critical parts of the tank.

February 8, 1945

Direction west. Back to the Westwall (Siegfried Line), the old Hindenburg Line of World War I. Our briefing tells us that the line is only partially occupied, but the pillboxes with protruding 88mm guns, bunkers, tunnels and tank traps look formidable. The American 1st Army in the north has had a terrible time (29,000 lives lost!!) at the Huertgen Forrest part of the Siegfried Line. In our sector, higher command has called for an artillery barrage on the defense line, and for 2 days the XIX Tactical Air force has been dropping bombs. Even when we don't hear the bombs, we can feel the earth shaking. To make matters worse, the Sauer River has flooded, which makes our approach more difficult.

February 14, 1945

We're through the Siegfried Line! Actually, it was far easier than we imagined, when one considers the difficulties encounter by the First Army (Gen. Hodges) in the north. The 324 lost only 6 tanks from pillbox fire, against which the M-4(75) and the M-4 (76) tanks were not too effective. The satchel charges of the infantry were more successful, as were the infantry mortars. Thank God for our infantry. One never appreciates their value until one comes to situations like this. Our replacement Sherman M-4 (76) are arriving daily. Soon, half our tanks will be M-4 (76)'s.

March 20, 1945

Direction west. We've come to the Rhine River at Coblenz, Germany and our job is to cross it. General Hodges (1st Army) has made his crossing at the unexploded General Ludendorff Bridge at Remargen, south of Cologne, but we need our own bridge. May I be forgiven for saying it, but the river looks so wide and so fast flowing. How on earth can we ford it? But Julius Caesar did so, and so can we. But Caesar didn't have German Me 262 jet planes flying overhead. So what? We have the 150th Combat Engineer Battalion to build us a treadway pontoon bridge, God bless them! This evening, I sent for my company commanders and impressed on them the importance of keeping up with the bereavement letters for the families of the men in their company who died in the heat of battle or elsewhere. it is easy to forget about our obligations to the families. And if something happens to the company commander (Heaven forbid!), the letters may not get written, and sooner or later, it's me, *moi!* who gets the blowback.

March 22, 1945

Direction west. The III Army has constructed its own pontoon bridge at Oppenheim, with another bridge to follow; and already some of the Allied tanks are making their way across. The 5th Armored Battalion (incl. the 324 Tanks) was also ordered to proceed to Oppenheim, Germany and make the crossing. We are now across the Rhine in Germany.

March 25, 1945

Darmstadt taken. Heavy fighting. Lost 4 tanks with their crews.

March 27, 1945

Patton sent a 300-man rescue party to Hammelburg, to rescue the US prisoners of war, including his son-in-law. The rescue party from the 4th Armored division (Lt. Col. Abrams) failed, and some were captured. Twenty-eight died. Patton could have written this up as a scouting party or a reconnaissance with force, but instead called it "a rescue party that went wrong" and accepted all criticism. I hope that when my turn comes, I'll have the guts to do the same.

March 28, 1945

Direction west. Just when we think that enemy resistance is fading, we encounter stiff opposition in the next town. Where the 4th Armored Tank Battalion spearhead encounters stiff resistance, they bi-pass the position and leave the cleaning-up to the rest of the column (which is us). Meanwhile, they keep moving.

I'll say this. The 4th Armored (Creighten Abrams) is the fastest moving tank brigade we have, and so say we all.

March 29, 1945

Frankfurt on the Main taken after 4 days of heavy fighting. The infantry have done a marvelous job battling the hand-held anti-tank weapons, which are a constant danger to tanks within a city. I had hoped to see the Goethe House, where Goethe lived as a young man, but they tell me it was destroyed.

April 5, 1945

We arrive in Kassel where we encounter fierce resistance. Fighting in the cities differs from fighting in the countryside. Before we can send in our tanks, an approach must be made for them by artillery and air support. Once in, the tank is dependent on the infantry to clear out the adjacent buildings; otherwise their position would be untenable. It's one thing for my M-4's to be hit by a self-propelled 75mm Pak 40 (Sf) at a distance of 1000 yards; and another to be disabled by a 70-year-old man, darting out of a building, holding a hand-held anti-tank weapon.

April 7, 1945

Direction west. We come to towns where the mayor stands outside the town hall, dressed in formal clothing, with a bright silk band around his waist. Since most mayors were more or less appointed by the Nazis, we show him little respect. The military government man usually orders that the town jail be emptied and the prisoners freed. Most of the prisoners are being held for some infraction of Nazi regulations. Occasionally we come to a farm where a concealed tank will open fire. We make short work of tank and farm and move on.

April 9, 1945

Direction west. We pass through towns with white flags hung from the windows. The soldiers have a saying: the larger the white sheet, the bigger the Nazi. On the other hand, when they see an overturned farmer's wagon on the road, my men got out of their tanks and lift it up.

April 11, 1945

Direction west. The opposition is often old men or boys, but their hand-held anti-tank weapons can be deadly. Unless they hold their hands up where they can be seen, our tankers do not give an approaching German soldier the benefit of a doubt, We lost two tanks in Kassel from unsuspected attacks by young, innocent-looking German soldiers who caught us unawares with their concealed *panzerfausts*. We travel slowly—20 miles a day—so that our supplies can keep up with us.

April 13, 1945

Direction west. Rumor has it that Patton wants to direct his army toward Berlin, but that SHAEF has turned him down.

April 14, 1945

Saw my first American T-24 heavy tank called the Pershing, which has a 90mm gun, matching the 88 mm on the Tiger; but much more nimble now, when we no longer need it.

April 16, 1945

Direction west. We came to Bayreuth, where we were halted for 3 days by a fierce SS detachment. Beyreuth is where the Wagner lovers draw inspiration. On the third night of our stay, my men slept in a cluster of outbuildings on the outskirts of the city, and I was billeted in a handsome private home nearby. A servant opened the door and showed me to my room. Dinnertime, I went down to the dining room to eat my rations, mixed with whatever else the kitchen had prepared.

The owner appeared and took her place at the table. She was a tall, aristocratic woman with thin lips. She had dressed for dinner in an evening gown, which was worn presumably for my benefit. Apart from an occasional word, we ate in silence.

After dinner, she sat at a piano and played a few romantic folk songs. Atop the piano was a rather old picture of her and her husband in civilian clothes, standing in front of the house. When she left the room to fetch the cognac, I went to the piano chair and lifted the seat. Hidden below the music was a framed photograph of the two of them, he in SS uniform standing outside a camp with the words over the gate: "Work makes (last word illegible)." From my Berlin days, I remembered that the words "Work makes free" appeared over the entrance to the concentration camps. Her husband must have been an SS officer stationed at a concentration camp, and she was paying him a visit. I put the picture on the piano, retrieved my kit and walked out. I should have realized from the house and servant. I shudder to think that at one time she would not have bothered me.

April 23, 1945

Direction west. At Asch, we encounter stubborn resistance which our tanks overcame, with a welcome assist from the air force. The same day, we liberated the Floessenburg concentration camp and I saw, for the first time, a sight no sane person could have imagined. Even now, I cannot think of it or write it down. They say that as hideous as these camps are, they do not compare with the 7 extermination camps the Soviets encountered in Poland. One of our military affairs officers told me that

Admiral Canaris had been a prisoner here and was executed three hours before our troops arrived.

April 25, 1945

Today we arrived at the border near Pilsen, Czechoslovakia and were ordered to halt. I had been looking forward to entering Prague and visiting my friend, Kubis, if still alive.

April 26, 1945

Direction north. Reached the Danube River near Regensburg, Austria. On the other side we saw a swarm of Soviet soldiers, celebrating. They were a reconnaissance company that had floated down the Danube from Vienna. They kept waving to us, inviting us over. A few rubber boats were brought up, and dozens of our troops crossed over. The celebrations were in full swing, with bottles of vodka circulating. Our troops also made a sizable contribution. The dancing and singing began, and the Russian women soldiers began their lively folk dances, which added to the merriment.

I crossed over, but stood apart from the party, as a good officer should. Not far away, I saw a Soviet officer watching the festivities, so I walked over and saluted. His name was Major Alexi Federoff, a former instructor at Moscow University, and he spoke perfect English. He was the son of a literature professor and a great fan of William Faulkner, whom I had never read. When I asked if I could do anything for him, he replied that he would be pleased to receive any work of William Faulkner I could find. The address was tricky. The one he gave me was the address of the adjutant of his brigade. Since the adjutant cannot read English, the book will be automatically turned over to the major for "examination."

We talked for two hours while he described his experiences in the army. Evidently, he has pleased his superiors, since they want him to remain in the service, rather than return to university life.

[The last days of the Third Reich. In accordance with the Yalta Agreement, Germany will be divided into 4 sectors: the east (Soviet); south (U.S); west (France;) and north

(Britain). Berlin, likewise, will be divided into 4 zones.]

May 8, 1945

GREAT REJOICING!! Germany has surrendered unconditionally!! Hitler is dead! Berlin is in ruins!

May 10, 1945

The 324 Combat Tank Regiment has been assigned temporary military government duty, and I have been designated Temporary Military Government Officer. To keep the men occupied, I gave them tactical training exercises, under our executive officer, Major Ted Crosby They explore the countryside for ammunition dumps, and in their free time, they hunt deer. The non-fraternization order is in effect ($65 for an infraction) but not vigorously enforced.

May 12, 1945

A point system has been posted to establish priorities for the return and discharge of the 3 million American soldiers now in Europe.

Most of my men have the points, of course, and are merely awaiting word to report to a designated embarkation port. Discipline has slackened elsewhere, and I hear that, in some units, trouble-makers stoke the soldiers' anxieties by telling them that the army plans to ship them to the Pacific. At the embarkation ports, some soldiers ignore their officers and mill around aimlessly, convinced that someone in high authority is preventing them from going home. General Eisenhower has been very lenient with these troublemakers—too lenient from my point of view.

So far, the 324 Tank Regiment has hung together and is patiently awaiting word to travel to whatever embarkation port is selected.

May 15, 1945

The port of embarkation for the 324 Tank Regiment will be Camp Lucky Strike, outside of La Havre, France. Men who lack sufficient points are being deployed to the Pacific, where the war with Japan is still under way. We receive directives to encourage enlistments, and a number of the old hands have signed on, but most of our future Army of Occupation will come from the States.

September 20, 1945

The American Occupation is hard at work, helping to restore power and electricity and repair water supply, sewerage, bridges and roads. A monumental task, but nothing beyond the capabilities of the U.S. Army.

October 3, 1944

Word has reached us that General Patton has been removed from command of the III Army in Bavaria and put in charge of the XV Army, which is a mythical unit with no troops. The reason, they say, is that he has been acting queerly. He always did act queerly, but this time he went too far, calling for war with the Soviet Union (while the American Army in Europe is rapidly disintegrating); and refusing to properly de-Nazify Bavaria. A professor sent by the military to investigate found dozens of well-known Nazis in important positions in the occupation government; also shocking neglect of the displaced persons in Patton's sector. I feel sorry for the old guy, but glad he's relieved of active command.

October 23, 1945

Questionnaire received from the War Department inquiring whether, for my next tour of duty, I prefer the Pacific or occupation duty. I checked off the occupation duty, and, in the appropriate space, mentioned that I spoke German and know Berlin well, having served there two years as military attaché.

November 4, 1945

I have been giving careful thought to retiring from the Army and going to graduate school. I discussed this by letter with Professor Joseph Collins of the Chemistry department at the University of Michigan, whose son, Norman, is a lieutenant in the 324. He suggested that instead of English literature, which I favored, that I study German literature instead, which has been sadly neglected since the onset of hostilities.

December 5, 1945

When I can, I spend weekends at an old inn, about 15 miles from the base, and out of reach of the GI's. A woman physician at the nearby Ebert Klinic named Johanna ("Hansi") Mann, has been kind enough to take me around and show me the countryside. This afternoon, we were seated on the patio of the inn. From inside, came the sound of the local singing club, practicing some old German folksongs. They sounded awful, and I paid them little attention, until they came to Schubert's *Linden Tree*, which they continued to massacre.

I realized then that suppressed within me was a desire to return to Berlin, the city which I have been avoiding; the city which had brought me so much joy and so much sorrow. Does the linden tree still stand in the churchyard, I wonder?

December 9, 1945

General Patton has died in a road accident. Let's say he was a great field commander, and let it go at that.

December 25. 1945

C-rations.

March 3, 1946

Still the often-chaotic behavior of troops on the way home for discharge. This afternoon I received orders addressed to Brigadier General Brian Manning ordering me to Berlin, to assume the duties of Deputy Commander for the Berlin garrison/US Zone.

March 4, 1946

A Major Mark Dinwiddy will relieve me tomorrow. Tonight, the few remaining officers from the 324th Tank Regiment gave me a farewell dinner. I tried not to make my speech sound maudlin. I thanked them for their service and wished that I could offer a toast to the 324 Tank Regiment, but I can't even do that, since they know I don't drink; so all they can get from me is my thanks for a job well done. And with that, I sat down.

DEPUTY COMMANDANT

March 5, 1946

The plane took off in early morning and reached the middle runway at Tempelhof Airfield in Berlin in 21/2 hours. It taxied to the military terminal, where an American honor guard awaited the new second in command.

Without doubt, they were the worst honor guard that could be imagined. Sloppy uniforms, badly needed haircuts and shaves—name it. I told their commanding officer, Captain Tom Black, that I would be back this afternoon and wanted to see improvement. Any man who gives him trouble, I want shipped out! Berlin is regarded as preferred duty by the enlisted men, and I want it kept that way.

A jeep was waiting for me outside the terminal. As we drove through the streets in the American zone, I saw indescribable destruction. Almost every building we passed had some damage, and many, like the American Embassy, were completely destroyed; but the streets had been cleared of debris and traffic flowed.

We came to the US Command in NW Berlin in the old I.G. Farben building. The soldiers on the sidewalk gave me a cursory salute and let me walk past them, but the two soldiers standing guard outside the building had seen the star on the jeep and presented arms. I walked into the small lobby and saw a crowd of idle soldiers and civilians. There was no cry of "General Officer!" but they did give way as I walked into the office of the Commanding Officer, General Frank Barker.

Four steel desks caught my eye, each occupied by a non-com dressed in different attire—one without a jacket, the other with sleeves rolled up, the other absent a tie, the fourth with shoes under his chair. A small fifth desk was occupied by a civilian. A Master Sergeant stood up and greeted me. I told him that I was going back out the door and when I came back in, he was to greet a general officer, like he had been taught.

I went out and returned to a cry of "General Officer!" One man had even rolled down his sleeves. The M/Sergeant then led me to my Deputy Commander's office. I listed from memory the infractions I had seen and told him he had a day to clean up this stable or out he'd go. Henceforth, the Berlin detachment has no room for a slovenly appearance!

There were papers piled up on my desk. I stacked them and told the M/Sergeant to sort them out, while I was gone. Back at Tempelhof Airfield, the situation had only slightly improved. Perhaps it was too soon to expect change, but at least the Captain has some idea of the poor quality of his men's performance. It was imperative, beginning immediately, that the Commanding Officer and any visiting dignitaries be properly greeted.

Returning to my office, I asked the S/Sergeant about the civilian who occupies the small desk and was told that it was our interpreter, Eugen Brunhofer, since none of our office personnel spoke German. The face looked familiar, but the name wasn't. The pile of papers on my desk had disappeared and instead, the S/Sergeant placed a page in front of me—one at a time, with a running commentary—all to be read and some to be signed. On a large wall map he showed me the different zones allotted to the four nations. There was also a depiction of the areas of bomb damage. I was happy to see that my own home in Bluecher Street lay in the French zone and that the area had been spared excessive damage.

S/Sgt Snider drew up my schedule. No need to report to my superior officer, since General Alfred Barker, the Commandant, was away in Washington. Tomorrow, courtesy calls should be made to the British and French commandants. After, I was scheduled to attend one of the twice-weekly meetings with the Soviets.

I told M/Sgt Bormann that I will be billeted in a private home on Bluecher Street in the French sector and gave him my address and the old telephone number. He consulted a map and then a notebook, before assuring me that the house had electricity, water, sewerage, and telephone service.

After a few hours of desk work, I had my driver load six days rations into the jeep, and we set off for home. Everything looked different. The old and haughty Berlin was gone, and the many victory statues had sustained damage to their figures or their pedestals. We were able to follow the old tram tracks out of the Centrum toward the outskirts. The streets had been cleared of rubble, all the way to the end of the line. There, the bomb damage began to lessen, and the area became recognizable. With gloomy misgivings, we came to Bluecher Street.

Our neighbor's house overflowed with a mob of mothers with damaged baby carriages, and idle men lounging about. The driver explained that the city compelled the home owners to take in families that had been bombed out.

At my first look at my home, my heart thumped. No crowds. The grass had been cut, the bushes trimmed, the shutters opened. and the black-out masking removed from the windows. But the window frames could use fresh paint and one of the upper-story windows had a cracked pane. I knocked, and Bruno opened the door. When he saw the uniform and then the face, he stood paralyzed, then stepped back and with a hallow croak, called to Resi. Her face had aged, and her hair was now all grey. Bruno eased a chair behind her. It took time before they could speak intelligibly, but when they did, the words bubbled out.

In short, Paul had been wounded and last they knew he was a prisoner in a Soviet field hospital. Fred had been compelled to join the German Army, and is now a prisoner of war at a British internment camp near Hanover. Caterine is upstairs in bed. She has been ill and is eating poorly, as is the case with Albrecht, the ash man, who also will not eat. Toward the end of the war, Bruno and Albrecht were compelled to join the Volksturm militia, and both managed to slip past the Russians to avoid capture.

My driver brought in the provisions. Resi made tea, and carried up the tray to Caterine's room. I had her go in first to let Caterine know who was standing outside, ready to beat down the doors to see her.

I entered the room, and approached the emaciated figure. Time had weighed heavily on her but still the soft, gentle features. She lay crying without a sound escaping from her lips. I kissed her cheek and her forehead, and whispered to her that everything will be well, if she would only eat and get her strength back.

I left Resi struggling to feed the patient and had my driver bring my bag to my room. Then I went down to the cellar to see Albrecht, whose chief trouble was, I suspect, that he had stopped eating, so that the others could have a larger portion.

March 6, 1946

Morning was spent with courtesy calls to the French Commandant, General Mattias Arsenault. He was especially friendly and delighted that my home was in his sector. He assured me that he was "at my service."

Then a visit to the Soviet Command in a grey lifeless building not far from the Brandenburg Gate. The soldiers surrounding the building wore baggy uniforms, but otherwise gave a snappy military appearance.

I entered the conference room, holding a list of the American GI's who had been arrested in the Soviet sector for drunkenness and the like, and my opposite number, in turn, was expected to present me with the list of Soviet prisoners resting in the Allied jails. We were then supposed to argue about which side caused the most damage and arrange an appropriate monetary settlement, which, by mutual agreement, was never excessive.

Once inside, I saw the familiar face of Alexi Federoff, now a colonel. He had known of my appointment and now saw my astonishment and offered a furtive smile. I realized quickly that he wanted to keep our friendship secret. He introduced himself, we presented lists and argued in English about the infractions.

When we had finished our business, he brought me up date. The decision had been made for him to remain in the Army and, like me, receive the appointment of Deputy Commandant for the Soviet garrison in Berlin. The books I had sent him had arrived, and he would be so thankful if I could find more of William Faulkner's work, since he had been waiting for years to read them. If I could send the books to the office of the Commanding Officer, they will end up on his desk.

I was unsure whether to mention my problem now, or wait, but decided to go ahead. I told him about Paul and his wounds. Does he think Paul could be transferred to some medical facility in Berlin? It would spare the Soviets of further medical costs.

He thought a while, then copied down the particulars: rank, unit, hospital, etc. He summoned his assistant and asked him to inquire about the unit Paul had served with. A half-hour later the assistant returned and reported. Alexi translated as the assistant read from his notes. Von Manig had shown no brutality towards his prisoners of war and had behaved decently to the partisans. According to secret Communist records, he was known to be a long-standing anti-Nazi, who had opposed Hitler from 1933. Not just after Stalingrad, like most of the other German officers. Alexi said that he would be happy to do what he could for Paul, but it may take time.

We left the Soviet Command Center and travelled to the British sector. The guard was small, but well turned out. In the commandant's office, I introduced myself and inquired of

Colonel Sir William Scott-Comfort. The commandant knew of him and informed me that Sir William had died while travelling from Lisbon to Britain when his plane was shot down over the Bay of Biscay.

The preliminaries concluded, I explained that I have a 15-year-old nephew (actually, second cousin) in a British POW camp and gave him the particulars. He offered to do what he could. The British were not as deeply immersed in the degasifications process as were the Americans, so that POW processing went faster.

I next visited the German Commercial Bank. The building was virtually undamaged, which is more than can be said for the adjacent structures. The interior was almost empty. Only one teller conducted business. To reach the director's office, I walked up the single flight, since the elevator was out of order.

Weisbart had aged but still had the broad smile and a hearty handshake. We exchanged news and pleasantries before I got down to the purpose of my visit. I told him that the American command was making The German Commercial Bank the official cashier for the GI checks. Also, the Finance Corps has been instructed to deposit all non-working funds in his bank. Also, his bank can now use the designation "Official Bank of the US Army/Berlin." Written notification will be sent him.

He was dumbfounded. I left before he could smother me with thanks.

March 14, 1946

The past 8 days have passed quickly. There have been many improvements, for which I can pride myself. Public services are being restored, more so than in the eastern (Soviet) sector, which lacks motivation, not ability. The American military police patrol conscientiously, and no longer spend their time in the taverns. The honor guard has begun to shape up (but still has a long ways to go), the American soldiers behave properly in public, saluting all officers domestic and foreign, and the office staff looks like an Army staff should look. Quite a change, but only the beginning.

As I walked into the outer office, I keep passing that civilian interpreter. Where had I seen him before? Then it came to me. He was the fellow who stole the furniture from the Goldbergs in the von Manig building! What was his name? Name? "Dieter Slichter." And who did he work for? The Gauleiter of Berlin.

I had my S/Sergeant fetch the *"Nazi Register/Berlin"* where they list the disclosures of the de-Nazification agencies. There was no appropriate listing for Slichter or Brunnhofer, nor anyone with that name who had worked for the Gauleiter of Berlin. Then I sent the S/Sergeant over to the Russians to confer with one of the English-speaking office personnel. Sure enough, they had an alert out for a Dieter Slichter, previously employed by the Berlin Gauleiter. Perfect!

After arming myself with a .45 Colt, I asked for an interpreter to go with me to the Russian zone. Slichter looked a little pale, but he came along and followed me up the stairs to the Commandant's office. I turned Slichter over to the Soviet MP's. and was tempted to convey to him regards from the Goldbergs. He probably didn't remember the name, but I did.

March 20, 1946

We took off from Tempelhof Airfield in a British C-47 and flew in pleasant weather to an airfield outside of Hanover. A duty officer had received an alert from the British commandant in Berlin and provided a jeep and driver to take me to their POW camp at Hildesheim. By now, the snow had melted, and the weather had turned warm. The camp was gigantic, far larger than can be imagined, with the interior divided into segments separated by strung barbed wire. There was a shabby two-story command building outside the compound, where the British version of the de-Nazification commission held its enquiries. I presented myself and my papers to the CO, who had his staff search the rolls for the name of the prisoner and his confinement sector.

As we approached the holding area, a voice in German boomed over the loudspeaker ordering Private Frederick von Manig to report to the entrance of his sector. A faint chorus of cat-calls followed the announcement. I followed the British officer until we came to the sector.

A young soldier with his back to me seemed to be scanning the camp.

When he turned towards me, he shrieked, "Oncle!" and threw his arms around me. I hugged him and lifted him off his feet as I used to do, only he was bigger and heavier now.

We hugged each other for several minutes before talking. How do you feel? Fine. How is the camp? Bad, but not too bad. When I told him that I was trying to have him released, he refused my help, saying that he would remain with his comrades. I smiled to myself. Only 3 months in the Amy, and already a grizzly veteran. Anyway, he was due to appear before the de-Nazification commission within the week and would then be released.

A Sergeant slouching on the ground got up, picked up my cap which had fallen off and handed it to me. He said that he lives in Berlin and would see that Fritz got home safely.

March 22, 1946

Alexi sent me further word about Paul. His brigade had been captured, He had been badly wounded from a high explosive shell burst, the fragments entering the right lung. and he had undergone emergency surgery at the Russian field hospital. After surgery, he was sent to a convalescent camp where he is now.

About transfer to a Berlin hospital, the Soviets will certainly not pay for additional medical expenses, but if the family wants further hospitalization, the patient can be discharged and sent to a Berlin facility.

March 28, 1946

Thanks to Alexi, the arrangements for Paul's release were far easier than I had expected and went faster. We met the train and had the patient transported immediately to the Charite Hospital; and, at the recommendation of the admitting doctor, to a medical service. How I miss Felix Cardenas. Paul is worn out and aged, like the rest of us.

March 30, 1946

Fred is home and has been to see his father, but before his visit, we made him change into his high school clothing. He has returned to Mrs. Robinson's school, which is still in operation, and, like Mrs. Robinson herself, is still going strong.

What do I do about an American flag? As Deputy Commandant, I should post the flag outside my home, but my neighbors might not be happy to see it outside the residence of a highly respected German general, as Paul has come to be regarded. ("He's being kept a prisoner!") So, I settled the matter by removing the flag and having Resi paste a small paper cut-out of the American flag alongside my name on the name register outside the entrance, This seems to have settled the matter and satisfied everyone.

April 4, 1946

Word has reached us that President Truman will be stopping over briefly in Berlin. This means intense preparations, most especially for the honor guard. The limousine tour of the city must be carefully planned, with provisions for sudden changes of venue, should the necessity arise. So far as I can determine, the secret for avoiding trouble is for the motorcade to proceed swiftly with as few scheduled stops as possible. We have 5 days to prepare. At one stop, we arranged to have a little boy holding an American flag. The President's car will stop; the President will say a few words to him for the benefit of the cameras; then the procession will move on.

April 10, 1946

The President has come and gone. The whole stop-over went like clockwork. The motorcade followed the schedule precisely, and there were few detours. At the end of the stop-over, General Peter Morris, in the President's party, complemented my chief, General Barker, on the meticulous preparations. Gradually our men are beginning to realize that Berlin is a show case theater. Even the honor guard performed tolerably well, but they have a long way to go before they satisfy me.

April 16, 1946

Paul has not greatly improved. He still runs a low-grade fever and coughs. Professor Dr. Mahler tells us that he needs a full course of penicillin, which his clinic does not have, nor do any of the Berlin hospitals. The American Army Hospital at Mannheim has the penicillin, but how do I get Paul there? The US Army hospitals are for US personnel and dependents. Is Paul a dependent?

He is mentioned as a dependent in the revised Manning Trust, so I telephoned Desmond Everett White II, explained the situation and asked that he prepare a brief to establish dependency and that he send it back as quickly as he could.

April 20, 1946

I showed the Manning brief to the Judge Advocate's office and requested a ruling as soon as possible.

April 21, 1946

The Judge Advocate made a weak argument for a dependency, but warned that it may later be challenged and overturned. Later? Who cares?

April 23, 1946

Paul was transferred today by US Army plane to Mannheim, together with his records, which I had translated into English, so that the intravenous treatment could begin promptly. Not thousands, but millions of units of penicillin daily. The bacteria don't have a chance.

May 21, 1946

Paul is home and he looks wonderful. He had to undergo three long courses of intravenous antibiotics, and the fluid in his chest has disappeared completely. Caterine is walking on air. She is up and about, and Resi Geulen persuaded her to visit a beauty salon in Potsdam before Paul came home. It was almost like the years have rolled away.

May 26, 1946

My thoughts keep returning to Elisabet, whom we do not discuss at home. Last night I saw her in a dream. She had slipped off a cliff and was falling through the air. I ran to the bottom and tried to catch her, but she fell through my arms and landed lifeless on the rocks, I woke up gasping for breath.

June 1, 1946

Director Dr. Weisbart gave me the name of a responsible funeral director, Wiedemann, by name. His office was south of the Tiergarten, in a little street with damaged homes and a few commercial properties. Mr. Wiedemann welcomed me with evident curiosity. I began by relating the relevant fragments of Elisabeth's tragic story, told him about the arrest, gave him the dates and handed him the non-informative letter that Caterine had received from the Gestapo.

I explained that I wanted the body reburied in the French cemetery. He thought a while, then replied that he may be able to procure the Gestapo records, which are surprisingly thorough for such a sinister organization. We may also learn the cause of death and the place of burial, provided that she had not been cremated; but he doubted I will be able to bury her in the French cemetery. For one thing, it is in the French sector; The civil authorities there frown on further city burials. They want the cemetery moved outside the city and the ground reclassified for building. Besides, the church authorities may not allow a burial, nor may the French commandant.

Undaunted, I asked him to begin his investigation and gave him a retainer. This quest has left me weary and exhausted.

June 4, 1946

Since my arrival, murders among US military personnel have declined, arrests are down, and drunkenness has been reduced. Services have been restored to an additional 31.5% of the households in the American sector since my arrival. My boss, General Barker, has received a letter of commendation from C-I-C, SHAFE in Heidelberg. Even the Berlin newspapers complement us on the return of law and order.

June 6, 1946

Wiedemann telephoned to report that he has located the grave site within a 97% probability. He awaits instructions about the burial arrangements.

The church has been closed for two years since that ill-fated air raid that inflicted the damage. The graveyard was hopelessly overgrown, but it seems to have had no ill effect on the linden tree, which, if anything, had grown since I last saw it. The tenants of an adjacent home gave me the pastor's address, which was a small cottage nearby, kept by an old,deaf woman. The Pastor Belianger himself was ancient, and, too, had difficulty hearing. I spoke in French and reminded him of his parishioner, Dr. Elisabet de Talligny. I told him her fate, and he shook his head despairingly. Her one wish, I told him, was to be buried in the church graveyard under the linden tree at the far end of the burial ground.

He knew the site. He told me that the tree roots will make digging the grave more difficult and cited a dozen other obstacles. I promised that if he would give permission, I would pay for repairs to the chapel. In the end, he consented, but informed me that further permission must be obtained from the civil government and from the French commandant, since the burial grounds were in the French sector. The old man had worn me out. I left a handsome check for the repairs and went home to recover.

June 7, 1946

The French commandant's office was in a modest three-story building in the French sector. The parking lot in front was filled with motorcycles and jeeps; and thankfully, no *grosse* Mercedes. I had made an appointment to see General Mathias Arsenault and was shown into his office without delay.

He rose to greet me and offered me a glass of cognac, but remembered I had refused it during my previous visit. We got down to the reason for my visit, and he listened attentively. I told him about Elisabet, her birthplace in Lorraine, her family history, and her desire to be buried in the French cemetery. He knew about the repairs now underway at the French chapel.

He stopped me. Of course I have his permission, and he will ask the civil authorities for a civil exception. He asked to be notified of the funeral date and promised to attend.

Some uncertainty seemed to be troubling him. Finally, as I was preparing to leave, he asked me if I had ever considered a posthumous marriage to Elisabet?

Posthumous marriage? What in the world was that? He explained that in rare cases if a couple had planned to marry, but one of them dies in a war before the marriage ceremony, the other is allowed to proceed with a civil ceremony, subject to the subsequent approval by the President of the French Republic. This came about as a result of the 1,700,000 deaths of French soldiers in the First World War, which left behind so many broken hearts and strained circumstances. There was a special application form to be submitted, which, after a half-hour of diligent search, the General's secretary was able to find. The fact that Elisabet and I had exchanged rings and she wore hers on the ring finger of the left hand on significant occasions was carefully noted. The fact that I resided in the French sector was also important, as was the fact that Elisabet was born in Lorraine; and that General Arsenault was a close friend and comrade-in-arms of President Charles de Gaulle. If no civil authority can be found to perform the ceremony, the Commandant said that he would perform it himself.

Tears welled up. I started to thank him, but he cut me short. He told me that he has a brother, a priest, who runs an orphanage in Casablanca for the unwanted children of French soldiers. On four occasions, the American soldiers came to the home with good things to eat and toys to play with. The only time ever the children had seen such kindness. And who do you suppose was their commanding officer?

July 10, 1946

More than a month has passed, and all the repairs have been completed to the roof, floor, nave and the pews. The day has arrived for the burial ceremony and the posthumous marriage. Two dozen worshipers were in attendance and a scattering of French and American officers. Pastor Belianger had to be helped up to the pulpit, but when the sermon began, his voice was strong and resonated through the small chapel. I was in formal attire, as one would for a wedding. General Arsenault read the prescribed civil ceremony, replete with civilian phraseology. and pronounced us man and wife. Permission from American military authorities had not been required under these circumstances.

After, the coffin was brought to the churchyard and lowered into the prepared grave. The excavation must have been difficult, since a few of the tree roots still protruded into the grave site and would have to be further trimmed before the casket can be lowered. I gazed at the full green leaves, now beginning to blossom and the words of the poem came into mind, but for some reason, I could not remember them.

July 20, 1946

All this running around must have worn me out, and I begin to feel weak and fatigued. I went to the medical infirmary today, and had one of the physicians examine me. All he found were enlarged lymph nodes, but for safety sake, he ordered blood work and a chest x-ray.

July 21, 1946

The medical office telephoned me and asked that I come in to discuss the laboratory findings. Colonel Donald Winters, our chief physician, and another colleague were in his office and had me lie down on an examining table.

When they had finished their examination, Colonel Waters reported that they had found an abnormality in my blood. To confirm their finding, they were sending me to our major Army hospital in Mannheim, Germany for further study. I told them about the aseptic meningitis, but they weren't interested.

July 23, 1946

I arrived in Mannheim today for my first appointment. It was a large hospital, as large as any I had seen in the States. The halls were filled with Army and civilian doctors and nurses, speaking English, German and French and a half-dozen other languages. The receiving doctor read my reports and sent me for tests: first to the lab for further blood work, then to the x-ray department, and finally to the EKG department. After, I was told to return tomorrow to see Dr. Everett Severinghaus, the consultant.

July 24, 1946

Dr. Severinghaus saw me today and examined me. After, he sat me down and spoke to me. He told me that I have a virulent form of acute leukocytic leukemia. An occasional patient may last the year, but to most, death comes sooner. So far as treatment, there are all kinds of treatment. Most of the medicines are poisons. They kill the both diseased and the healthy tissue. My hair will fall out, my appetite will disappear, and I may last a few months longer than do the people without therapy.

August 26, 1946

At Sloan Kettering in New York, a bone marrow biopsy was performed. The same diagnosis, but they proposed a new treatment protocol that shows promise. Unfortunately, it may make me sick, and I will lose my hair. How long will the treatment prolong life? They have high hopes that it may stretch things out for six months. Meanwhile, a new cure may come along.

September 6, 1946

Mayo Clinic, 6 months, maybe.

September 12, 1946

At Walter Reed Army Hospital in Washington DC, they began the Medical Retirement Proceedings. I considered looking up the Bradfords and the Harmons, but was afraid my gaunt look might frighten them; or worse, that it may give Clayton nightmares.

September 17, 1946

On the way back to Berlin. Since I have not yet been terminated, I am still permitted to fly on the Army Air Corps flights.

September 19, 1946

Home. Everyone is doing well. Fred is back in school and will soon graduate. He has taken the Arbiter and College Entrance exam and has done well with both. Bright kid. He has not yet decided whether he would like to attend the

Berlin Institute of Technology or M.I.T. Caterine is up and around and has resumed most of her activities. Paul is quite active and has been called to Bonn for secret interviews. The American army foresees that within 5 years, West German sovereignty will be restored, and a new West German army will then be formed. Paul, who is regarded as having had genuine anti-Nazi credentials and who can now speak Russian, is young enough to be considered for high rank. Resi and Bruno Geulen feel well and even Albrecht is now quite active. Much as I would like to do so, it is still impractical to think of replacing our coal burning furnaces with an oil burner. Perhaps I'll reconsider when Albrecht is too infirm to care for both the furnaces and the landscape.

****

POSTLUDE

The following notice appeared on page 8A in the October 23, 1946 edition of the *Boston Post.*

The Director of the Manning Trust is saddened to announce the death of Brigadier General Brian Manning, USA (Ret.) on October 22, 1946 in Berlin, Germany, from cancer. The burial ceremony was conducted at the French Protestant Chapel in the French sector of Berlin, following which General Manning was buried alongside his wife, Elisabet *nee* de Talligny, whose posthumous marriage to General Manning had been previously sanctioned by the President of France.

ACKNOWLEDGEMENTS

I express my thanks to Andrew Ladenheim for his help in diligently unearthing facts and dates; Mrs. Jean Ganley helped spare me the ever-demanding desk tedia. I have read many books while preparing this manuscript, few more helpful than *Underground in Berlin*, by Marie Jalowicz; *Berlin Embassy* by William Russell; *The Nazi Officer's Wife*, by Edith Beer and Susan Dworkin; and *Marlene Dietrich* by Maria Riva.